Merlin's ™
Candles

L. B. MacDonald

ISBN 0-9731031-5-1

*Leap*Cloud Inc.

505 Rothesay Avenue, Suite #300
Saint John, NB
Canada E2J 2C6

www.merlinscandles.com

Merlin's Candles

L.B. MacDonald

Dedication

For my wonderful sons, Joshua and Ryan.

And for Peter Meades, who shared his love of reading with my son, Joshua. When I first met Peter, he was a Grade 6 student taking part in a "reading buddies" program with my son's Grade 1 class, but after Joshua told me that he liked to read because Peter had said that "reading was cool," I realized that Peter was really Merlin the Magician.

Acknowledgments

I would like to acknowledge with heart-felt gratitude the advice, guidance, help and encouragement that I received from the administration team and the teachers at Franklin Street Public School, Markham, Ontario:

> Jossett Sassoon, Principal
> Mary Louise Icely, Vice Principal
> Anetta Mastrangelo
> Marina Cochrane
> Jay Wolkoff
> Joan Miyata
> Hilda Hutton
> Lynn Girdler

I owe a debt of gratitude to Bette Walker (teacher/author/Language Arts consultant) for her considerable contribution to the editing of the novel and to the preparation of the teacher's kit.

A special thank you goes out to Jamie Boulding and Anne Feddick at the Strathcona Park Lodge in British Columbia for sharing their knowledge of the park with me — I particularly acknowledge Jamie Boulding's help in choosing the characters' route through the park. Also a special thank you goes out to Pam Krannitz, an environmental scientist in B.C. who provided invaluable feedback.

I would like to send a joyous thank you to all of the students who read the novel, in its various stages, and who gave me valuable and detailed comments and suggestions:

- Sarah Cassman (Grade 8), who was the novel's first reader;

- The students of Mrs. Cochrane's Grade 6 class (Franklin Street Public School)

- The students of Ms. J. Brown's Grade 7 class (Elmbank Junior Middle Academy).

I would like to thank my husband, Jim MacDonald, not only for the wonderful cover art he created for the book, but for his enduring love and support.

Prologue

Western Britain, AD 539

Morgan Le Fay watched the magical reflection of King Arthur's final battle in the shimmering depths of a large black stone. She smiled as Camelot fell.

Morgan was beautiful in her triumph. She stood, wrapped in a soft black velvet robe, twirling a golden necklace around her finger. At the end of the necklace hung a blood-red ruby encircled by a golden serpent with silver fangs. She stood in the centre of a gaping cavern: bony stalactites reached toward the ground; sparkling rivulets of water left glittering spider tracks on the rough walls. She stared into the dark glassy surface of the slab of polished obsidian beside her and watched as a king died and a sword was thrown back into a lake. The image rippled and vanished. Morgan smiled: satisfied. Her revenge was complete. She had killed Arthur — son of Uther Pendragon — son of the man who had killed her father. She lifted the amulet to her lips and kissed it. She looked up at Merlin and said, "I win."

The old magician blinked himself awake. He looked tired. His long gray beard was tangled, and his blue and gold robe was faded and torn. He felt funny, dizzy. Startled, he realized that he was looking down at Morgan from a great height. He tried to move. He couldn't. He was trapped in something soft, something sticky, something warm.

Morgan watched Merlin squirm. It had taken her years of watching, listening, learning and waiting to master enough magic to trap him. There was no way that he could break the cocoon of magic that held him. Morgan smiled a spider's smile and prepared to suck the last of Merlin's power, the last of Merlin's life, from his frail old body. She opened her arms wide.

A warning bell went off in Merlin's head. Quickly, he blurted out, "No, Morgan, you lose!"

Morgan opened her eyes. "Arthur is dead!" she shot at him. "And not even you, Merlin, can change that."

Merlin knew she was right. But he also knew that it was Arthur's life that mattered, not his death. And Morgan couldn't touch that. He cried out, "You will never be able to erase his memory. His deeds will shine like a beacon for all good men to follow."

Morgan waved away his words like so many gnats, "In a few years, Arthur will be forgotten," she said with a smile, "and so will you."

"Better make sure, Morgan," Merlin said. "Just in case."

Morgan Le Fay paused, her eyes narrowed, her smile faded. She spun toward the glassy black slab of obsidian where Arthur's image still lingered; she waved one hand over its translucent surface. "Show me — from this dead but once bright fulcrum — what through time and age will come . . ."

A small prick of light began to glow in the bottom left-hand corner of the volcanic rock. It flickered and dimmed. Morgan smiled. But the little dot of light did not go out. It steadied and grew stronger. Slowly, another ember joined it, then another, and another. With each new light, the previous one seemed to glow brighter. The sparks of light continued until they created a clear path across the darkness.

As Morgan watched, her surprise turned to anger. She knew that the lights represented Arthur's legacy. "This cannot be!"

Merlin whispered, "Beautiful, isn't it? Like a string of candles lighting the way to the future."

Morgan was furious. "Candles indeed!" she thought. Arthur had just been snuffed out — all should be darkness.

"Face it, Morgan," said Merlin. "There's nothing you can do. Killing Arthur didn't change anything."

Morgan froze — thinking, realizing, understanding. "You mean, now — killing him now, didn't change anything," she said. "But if I had killed him when he was a boy, before he pulled the sword from the stone . . . before the Lady of the Lake gave him Excalibur . . . before he united the warlords against the Saxons . . . before he built Camelot —"

"You cannot change the past, Morgan."

"I can't?" her voice was quiet and sly. "Why not?"

"Because I won't let you. I was Arthur's guardian from birth. I was his father's magician. I am present in every moment of your past."

Morgan stared at Merlin for a long moment. "Then I'll just have to kill you — when you were young. Before your magic was strong, before your meddling began!"

Merlin smiled. This was the moment he'd been waiting for. He looked again at the little lights sparkling across the black stone. Morgan's understanding of their situation was no deeper than the rock into which she stared. The black glass, like Morgan's dark plan, had been conceived in haste. Obsidian, Merlin knew, was formed when lava cooled too quickly. He knew that Morgan's desire for revenge would spur her to act with similar impatience.

Confident in her new plan, Morgan raised her hands, fingers aimed at Merlin's heart, "Without you, My father wouldn't have been murdered. Without you, my mother and I wouldn't have been driven from our home. Without you, I might have been a queen. Without you, Arthur would never have existed. Without you! All without you!" Morgan took a deep breath and closed her eyes.

With the whisper of velvet on stone, she began to whirl in a circle. Merlin looked at the ground beneath Morgan's spinning feet — he saw the spin of time. He knew, without

a doubt, that this was the moment — one mistake and everything would change. One mistake and he could have a
normal life. One mistake and there would be no King Arthur
— now or ever.

Merlin started to whisper, but Morgan didn't hear him.
Her laughter rose as the ground began to shake. Mist seeped
from cracks in the earth. Stalagmites erupted from the cavern
floor encircling her in a ring of stone. Morgan touched her
necklace, "To Merlin's youth, I fly with speed. When he was
young, to undo the deed!"

The stalagmites continued to grow and twist as Morgan
continued to spin. She was being dwarfed by the rising fingers of stone. A crack of lightning exploded upward from
the obsidian, and Morgan Le Fay disappeared in a zigzag
streak of electric blue frenzy.

Vancouver Island, 2003

The buildings of a little shopping plaza in Glen Lake, British Columbia stood silhouetted by the moonlight. A sudden
streak of summer lightning illuminated them for an instant
then left them to the dark. At the edge of an adjoining park,
a lump appeared. A lump of shadow that solidified into
velvet. Morgan Le Fay moaned with pain and fatigue. She
was exhausted.

As she rose to her knees, Morgan gazed at everything:
buildings, lampposts, storefronts, garbage cans — without
recognition. "What magic is this?"

With great effort, Morgan got to her feet. She stood, staring
at her unfamiliar surroundings. She knew she had travelled
to another time and another place. But exactly where — and
exactly when — was she? Morgan suddenly realized that
she knew very little about Merlin: she had no idea where he

had been born, where he had grown up, or how old he had been when his magical powers first emerged.

Morgan stumbled, caught herself, and took a deep breath. She needed rest. She looked around and found a hiding place in the centre of a large group of close-growing shrubs. Tomorrow, there would be time enough to get her bearings — time enough to ensure that a young man never grew old.

1

"You could help him," a calm voice whispered.

"What?" Michael Halsey turned from watching Trevor picking on some kid over by the swings to see Mr. John Merlin, his science teacher, standing behind him.

Merlin nodded toward the boy in the distance, "He needs help. You could help him."

"Me? I don't even know the kid!" Michael scowled and turned away from his teacher. He looked across the school-yard and saw the kid holding onto the chain link fence, as if it could protect him, as if it could hide him.

"Benny's a baby! Benny's a baby!" taunted Trevor.

The kid, Benjamin Lau, closed his eyes.

"Hey, 'baby Benny', you gonna run home to your momma?" Trevor teased.

Benjamin started to cry.

Michael couldn't take it. He looked away.

"You're strong," Merlin continued, bringing Michael back to the situation at hand.

"No, I'm not!" Michael said, "Trevor's way bigger 'an me! Besides, you're the teacher. You help him."

Merlin looked at his pupil and nodded; he understood that Michael was afraid. "If I help him," Merlin explained, "he'll be teased again tomorrow — only it will be worse. And I didn't say you were big. I said you were strong: inside, where it counts."

Michael felt uncomfortable, the way every kid did around Mr. M. A feeling like more was always expected of you. "Mysterious Mr. M." — that's what all the kids called him. He was too tall, too thin, too everything. Mr. M. looked like he was about thirty years old but he never talked about himself. Even his clothes kept his secrets. Mr. M. always wore the same pale blue shirt and gold corduroy blazer with the leather elbow patches. They always looked clean — some of the kids figured he had a closet full of them.

Michael was on the debating team and in the science club — both of which had the dubious honour of having Mr. M. as their faculty advisor. Thanks to him, Glen Lake Public School's debating team was known throughout Southern Vancouver Island as the "Silent Majority". Mr. M. usually spent the first half of any meet arguing with the judges about the topic to be debated. If he didn't think it was worth their time, he would pack-up his team and drive them home. Mr. M. believed that debating was about thinking, not talking. He wouldn't let his team waste their time talking about nothing. They spent a lot of time driving back and forth, discussing the merit points of debates not taken. Michael smiled, those times were the best: everyone on the team was all wound up and talked all at once — not like a debate at all.

The science club was the messiest, most dangerous place to be after school. The members were on a first-name basis with the school nurse, the local fire department, and the school's long-suffering janitor.

The thought of "long-suffering" made Michael turn back to look at the boy by the fence. He tried to shrug off the painful sight, "He'll be all right. Nobody's really hurting him."

"No?"

Michael wasn't sure if Mr. M. had spoken, or if he'd heard the reproach in his mind. "It's just words," Michael said, suddenly feeling defensive.

"Words have power." Merlin gestured toward the boy, "He is being hurt. He's in trouble, and he's in pain."

"How would you know?" Michael shot back, suddenly afraid he was being pushed into something.

"Because I've been him."

"Yeah, right." Michael looked from long and lean Mr. M. to the short, chubby and scared kid by the fence.

"When I was seven, I had to walk to school" Merlin began. "It wasn't far, but when you're seven, everything is far . . ."

As Merlin spoke, Michael closed his eyes, hoping the story wouldn't be too long, but glad to have his mind taken off Trevor and the boy.

"One day," Merlin continued, "some kids were waiting for me. They were holding hands in a chain that stretched across the sidewalk and the road."

Michael, his eyes still closed, imagined he could see the chain of children. He imagined every living link glowering at him. He tried to understand what was happening, what he had done, what he was supposed to do. For some reason, these children hated him, wanted to hurt him.

In his mind, Michael picked the weakest link and tried to break through the arms, but the hands seemed clasped in iron. He tried another link. Equally unbreakable.

As Merlin continued his story, Michael imagined the children pinching him, picking little holes in his clothing, calling him names.

Finally, Michael imagined one of the links breaking; he imagined himself starting to run. His heart raced. He'd never felt like this. He was angry, hurt, ashamed, and most of all, scared.

Michael's ears started to ring. A wailing sound grew and grew, filling his mind, pushing the bad feelings away and making him dizzy.

Michael opened his eyes and tried to catch his breath. All around him, kids were running toward the school. Somewhere, a bell was ringing.

Michael looked up at Mr. M. and realized it had only been a story. "Wow, the way you told that — I felt like I was really there."

"I told you words had power." Merlin turned and headed back toward the school.

Michael didn't follow. He needed a minute to clear his head. He looked over to the fence and saw that Benjamin was being gently led away by Mrs. Pearson, the shorter of the two short cafeteria ladies. Michael winced. Why did it have to be a cafeteria lady? Mr. M. was right. Tomorrow would be worse.

Michael picked up his back pack and hurried to class.

2

In the hall outside John Merlin's classroom, Mr. Carter, the gym teacher, and Mr. Singh, the music teacher, gave the door a wide berth.

"I wonder what the wizard's going to blow up today?" asked Mr. Carter.

"I don't care," answered Mr. Singh, "so long as he doesn't blow a hole in the floor. My room's right below his."

Inside the science lab, all eyes were trained on Mysterious Mr. M.

"Who can tell me what is in this test tube?" Merlin asked. He started to shake it, but stopped himself, as if afraid the contents might not take kindly to the agitation. "Remember, each question counts. The last class got it in five."

Merlin stole a glance at Michael, knowing his competitive nature. "Think," he continued. "Think hard. Phrase your question in a way that gets you the most information. Tiffany."

Tiffany Guzzmann went pale. She stood up, cleared her throat and whispered, "Is it smelly?"

Merlin's right eyebrow raised itself. The room grew silent.

"Uh, I mean, how smelly is it?" Tiffany amended.

Merlin's left eyebrow joined his right. Everyone held their breath.

"No, wait!" Tiffany said with inspiration, "What's it smell like?"

Merlin's eyebrows lowered themselves, and he nodded approvingly. He took the stopper out of the test tube, held the open end under Cory Buchner's nose, and waited.

Cory saw the test tube coming and stopped breathing. He looked left; he looked right. There was no help in sight. He looked pleadingly up at Mr. M.

Most of Merlin's compounds smelled horrible, others made you sneeze, some made you gag. Cory swallowed and took a tiny sniff: nothing. He sniffed again: again nothing. He took a deep breath, smiled and announced his discovery to the class, "Nothing! It smells like nothing!"

A few of the students laughed. At the back of the room, Michael groaned.

"Do you have a problem with the answer to Tiffany's question, Mr. Halsey?" asked Merlin.

"Uh, no," Michael sputtered. He didn't even have to look up, he could feel Mr. M.'s right eyebrow raising itself. He didn't need to wait for the left one to join it. Michael stood up, "It's just that we still don't know anything about it."

"Oh?" Merlin's ears seemed to be trying to join his eyebrows.

Michael couldn't watch; he looked at the floor and mumbled, "We wasted a question." Michael sat down.

"But you didn't," Merlin's calm voice intoned from above.

Michael looked up, startled. Mr. M. was standing right over him. Somehow, he'd made it down the aisle without a sound. And he was smiling.

"Sometimes, knowing what something isn't, tells you more about it than knowing what it is," Merlin said.

Michael rolled his eyes. Why was everything always so complicated when Mr. M. was involved?

"For example," Merlin turned and strode toward the front of the class, "if I say, 'Michael Halsey is not a king —'"

Mr. M. froze in mid-step, mid-word, mid-way up the aisle. His face went pale; his eyes grew wide; his knees began to buckle. His long, thin fingers lost their delicate grip on the test tube, and it fell toward the hard tile floor. The students nearest him dove for cover.

The test tube shattered. Bits of glass and granules of salt skidded and bounced innocently across the floor. Merlin caught the corner of a desk with one hand and covered his face with the other. He looked sick.

Michael was the first to reach him, "Mr. M., are you all right?"

Merlin's mouth had gone dry. He nodded and rasped, "Something bad . . . like a smell . . ."

Michael looked down at what was left of the harmless contents of the test tube.

"No," continued Merlin, noticing Michael's gaze. "In my mind . . . like a premonition." Merlin looked past Michael to the windows, through the glass, and into the distance. He had the most uncomfortable feeling that something bad was going to get him.

Amid the shrubbery, at the edge of the little shopping plaza, Morgan Le Fay sat up and rubbed her eyes. She felt refreshed — the sleep had done her good.

Peeking through the bushes, she surveyed the world before her. Men and women milled about, chatting with each other, carrying packages, going in and out of shops. Morgan paused. She knew she had travelled through time, but she hadn't expected to appear in such a strange and foreign land. Morgan decided to find out where she was. First, she needed information.

With casual grace, Morgan emerged from the bushes, smoothed her velvet robes, and took a seat on a nearby bench. Morgan studied the people as they walked past her;

she stared at the shop signs and tried to grasp their meaning. The bits of language she heard seemed vaguely familiar — something in the root of the words — but the sentences eluded her.

Across from Morgan, two women sat down on another bench. The older woman seemed to be arguing with the younger woman about something called a "salary". Morgan was familiar with the Latin word "salarium" meaning "salt allowance" — the part of a Roman soldier's pay that was supposed to be used to buy salt. Morgan listened closer, trying to understand the conversation. Yes, they were definitely talking about the younger woman's salt allowance — and just like most of the Roman soldiers Morgan had known, the younger woman had not spent hers on salt. The older woman insisted she should have "deposited" it in something called a bank. Morgan didn't know the word bank, but she could make a good guess about "deposited". "Positus" was Latin for "placed" or "put", and the prefix "de" commonly meant "away". The older woman had wanted the younger one to put her allowance away, probably in a safe place.

Morgan's natural confidence was returning. With a little magical help, she should be able to master the language of this place. She looked at the words printed on the boards outside the many shops. A particularly colourful sign read, "Bonny's Barter Basement". While Morgan didn't know who Bonny was, or what a basement was, she certainly knew the Gaelic words "brath" and "bradag" — they referred to thievery and taking advantage of others by unfair means. Well, If this Bonny thought she could get the better of Morgan in a trade, she was about to be surprised.

3

The last bell had rung, and John Merlin hurried down the hall, swept along on the tide of students toward the main doors. As he passed the principal's office, a figure emerged directly in his path.

"Oh, Ms. Sanchez," Merlin said, nearly stumbling into her, "I'm leaving a bit early. I'm not feeling well, and I have an appointment —"

"Yes. With me. Three hours ago." Selena Sanchez waved a permission slip in front of his face, "Field trips require one of these — from each student — signed by a parent or guardian."

"Oh, I'm sorry, I forgot — it was just a spur of the moment outing — we didn't go far."

Ms. Sanchez spoke through clenched teeth, "All of your 'outings' are on the spur of the moment. You must learn to plan, Mr. Merlin, plan. It is the key to success in life and in your career as a teacher, do I make myself clear?"

"Yes Ma'am. Uh, thank you," Merlin winced and looked toward the door.

"Honestly," thought Ms. Sanchez, "some teachers were worse than students."

Merlin nodded a quick farewell and hurried down the hall and out of the building.

Ms. Sanchez watched him, wondering if he was planning to call in sick tomorrow; he did look a little pale, and he was perspiring.

Morgan Le Fay was "dressed-to-kill" in a tight-fitting red dress. She'd had no trouble trading Bonny her luxurious robe for the dress, a matching shawl, and a large purse. She looked at her reflection in a store window, pleased. These fashions suited her — anyone meeting her would simply see a beautiful woman with long black hair in a stunning red dress. Morgan draped the leather bag over her shoulder; it now held the contents of her robe's many pockets — and the money Bonny had hastily added to the deal when it had looked like Morgan might change her mind.

The money had fascinated Morgan. She was familiar with coins, but the unusual substance of the "bills" (as Bonny had called them) intrigued her. The odd texture of the thin white sack Bonny had offered her was equally unfamiliar. Morgan kept the bills, but she didn't keep the "plastic bag" — something about it felt wrong, unnatural — like it had been altered somehow — internally — magically.

Morgan paused. This land was filled with magic: wagons that roared without horses, lights and sounds that seemed to come from nowhere, images in boxes of tiny people. Perhaps this place was the source of all magic. If so, it was fitting that Merlin had been born here, and fitting that he would die here.

Merlin lay on the couch, his arm thrown over his eyes, breathing deeply. It was cool here. Cool and quiet and safe.

Behind him, Dr. Cassandra Westinghouse sat waiting.

Finally, Merlin exhaled and said, "I had the strangest dream last night." He moved his arm away from his face and stared at the ceiling, "I dreamed that I was an old man, and I had been caught in a trap by a beautiful woman. I was dressed in long blue robes, and I was watching the image of a king fighting a losing battle."

Cassandra made a note.

"It was very real," Merlin added. "More like a memory than a dream."

"How did the dream make you feel?" Cassandra asked.

Merlin paused and thought about the question, "Lonely."

Cassandra made another note. Her voice was calm and soothing, "Anything else?"

Merlin covered his eyes again. "Today in class, I had the creepiest feeling that something was after me. Something bad."

"Bad?" Cassandra prompted.

"Dark, evil . . . I don't know."

"How do you feel now?" Cassandra asked.

Merlin stole a nervous glance at the window, "Like I'm running out of time."

Cassandra nodded and underlined something she'd written earlier.

Suddenly, Merlin sat up, turned to Cassandra and asked, "Did you think about it? Can we start today — right now?"

Cassandra's expression darkened.

Merlin added with great emotion, "You don't understand how important this is to me!"

"I do understand, and you know how I feel about hypnosis."

"But you've seen it done; you know how to do it."

Yes, but I don't believe you'll find what you're looking for."

Morgan Le Fay stood staring at the phone booth, wondering what it was. She would have lumped it in with the many other unexplained curiosities of this place and passed it by — except for the book. Books were rare and valuable. Morgan knew that some books had power. This one had a shrine!

Carefully, she approached the booth and gingerly touched the book with one finger. Nothing. No magic guarded it. Still, she whispered a few words of protection before opening it.

Names. Rows and rows of names. Morgan didn't know what to make of it, but she wasn't going to discount it until she'd checked for one name in particular.

There it was — all alone: the only Merlin in the book, and beside it, numbers and words. Morgan focused her mind and concentrated. The first number and word were a location. The significance of the second set of seven numbers eluded her. But that didn't matter, a location was what she wanted.

Dr. Cassandra Westinghouse studied her patient. She didn't believe in giving false hope. "I must warn you, John, you can't find memories where there are none," the tone of her voice was gentle although she knew her words were not. "Your records say your mother gave you up at birth. You were raised in a series of foster homes before you were finally adopted. Your father wasn't even listed on your birth certificate."

"I know, but there has to be more to me than my mother's last name. She was a real person —" Merlin looked away, "a person who probably had a really good reason for giving up her son."

Cassandra softened her voice even more, "I'm sure she had a good reason, and I'm sure she loved you."

Merlin looked up into her kind face and whispered, "Please?"

Cassandra knew what he was asking. She thought for a moment then nodded her head. Satisfied, Merlin lay back on the couch and closed his eyes.

"You are calm," Cassandra began. "You feel content. You are enjoying a sensation that is almost like floating."

But Merlin didn't look content. He didn't look like he was enjoying anything, and he certainly didn't look like he was floating. The colour was draining out of his face, and he was beginning to perspire.

Cassandra noted his reaction with concern, "It's all right, nothing here can hurt you. You're calm, you feel — "

Merlin sat up, "It's no good. I can't concentrate."

Cassandra kept her voice quiet, even, "Relax, give it time."

"No. It's come back. That feeling I had today, that feeling that something's going to get me."

Cassandra reached for her notebook, "Describe it to me. Is it the same as before?"

"No. It's different . . ."

"How different?"

"Stronger."

"And?"

"It's like . . . like . . ." Merlin turned to look at Dr. Westing-house, "Have you ever had one of those feelings that's like a warning? You know, a premonition? Like when people change their mind about getting on an airplane because they suddenly get a feeling that it's going to crash — and later they find out that they did?

Cassandra shook her head, "No."

"But if you did?"

Cassandra paused for a long moment then answered succinctly, "I'd change my flight."

The streetlight outside Merlin's modest house on Windward Drive sputtered and died. A lone figure in a red dress stood amid the heavy shadows on the porch. Morgan Le Fay didn't knock; she didn't need to. Instead, she touched her necklace, pursed her lips and blew. The deadbolt crumbled into dust and the door swung open.

"Do you have laundry service?" Merlin asked as he signed the motel's register.

"Yes sir," answered the clerk, "I'll send someone to your room as soon as you're settled."

Merlin nodded and looked around at the sterile lobby of the Lakeside Motel. He agreed with Dr. Westinghouse — only he wasn't changing his flight, he was changing where he slept. Ever since this afternoon, he'd had the strongest feeling that he shouldn't go home.

Morgan Le Fay rummaged through Merlin's belongings for over an hour. She found much that was interesting but nothing she could use.

The small house was cozy, all warm earth-tones and soft throw-rugs. The library was the largest room, teeming with books full of numbers and compounds and plants.

Morgan was not surprised to find that Merlin had so many books. He'd always had a large collection. However, she was intrigued by the pages. They were made of the same strange material as the "bills" Bonny had given her; the same strange material as in the "Book of Lists" she'd encountered at the shrine. They felt crisp, not at all like Celtic parchment or Roman vellum — both of which were made from prepared animal skin.

Some of the books, Morgan understood; others, made no sense. Her comprehension in this new language was dependent upon those concepts she already knew. Morgan surmised that Merlin's magical abilities were beginning to emerge. But she wasn't worried. In his youth, he would be no match for her.

"Yoo hoo!" a voice called from the open front door.

Startled, Morgan's magic rose to her protection.

"Yoo hoo, anybody home?" Mrs. Fitz-Gardner called. She was a plump woman habitually dressed in pink. "Mr. Mer — Oh!" Mrs. Fitz-Gardner stopped when she saw Morgan.

Not feeling any threat coming from the woman, Morgan Le Fay relaxed.

"I'm sorry, I didn't mean to interrupt," Mrs. Fitz-Gardner said. "It's just that I noticed your cans weren't out."

"Cans?" repeated Morgan.

Mrs. Fitz-Gardner noticed Morgan's delicate and unusual accent. "Tomorrow's garbage day," she continued more loudly and slowly, assuming she was speaking to someone just learning English, "if you don't put them out, you'll be stuck with your garbage until next week."

Morgan stared at the woman and said nothing.

Mrs. Fitz-Gardner smiled uncomfortably, "Sometimes people forget; I'm just being neighborly." She noted Morgan's dress, her beautiful raven hair, her exquisite figure. She looked around the room and saw that it was lit only by candles. Her eyes opened wide with realization, "Oh!" she exclaimed, a little embarrassed, "I'll just be on my way — leave you two love birds alone." Mrs. Fitz-Gardner winked and turned toward the door.

"Wait," commanded Morgan. She touched her necklace.

The woman in pink froze.

"My friend, Merlin, is late. Do you know where he might be?" Morgan's liquid accent made the familiar words sound strange, unearthly.

"Well, he might still be at the school: a teachers' meeting or something," Mrs. Fitz-Gardner offered.

"School?"

"Glen Lake Public School, in the west end of Colwood, over by . . well . . . Glen Lake."

Satisfied, Morgan lifted her hand from her necklace.

Mrs. Fitz-Gardner swallowed hard, nodded a quick good-bye, and headed for the door at a near run.

"School." Morgan played with the word in her mind. She knew the barbarians would destroy the few remaining church-run schools that had risen in the wake of the Roman exodus. Without Arthur to repell the invaders, reading and writing would disappear all the faster. Good. Ignorant people were easier to control. Perhaps she would be Queen after all.

Morgan smiled. If Merlin liked school so much, he was about to get the lesson of his life!

5

It was only eight a.m., but already the playground was filling up with children. Behind a large western hemlock, a shadow stirred. Morgan Le Fay woke to the sound of chanting. "Benny's a baby, Benny's a baby."

She smoothed her dress and shook the dirt and grass from her shawl. Merlin had not shown up here, nor had he returned home last night. She blinked in the bright sunlight and looked for the source of the chanting.

Over by the basketball court, a small group of children stood in a semicircle around two boys. Trevor sneered, "Give it to me, Benny, or I'll shove your head down the girls' toilet."

Benjamin Lau held onto the slender basketball pole with one hand while he dug into his pocket with the other. "It's not fair." He held out his hand, palm up, displaying the money.

Trevor snatched the coins, "Oh, poor baby Benny, you gonna tell your momma?"

Benjamin shook his head.

Satisfied, Trevor turned to the small audience, but before he could gloat, he was interrupted by a small voice from the far side of the court.

"Give it back," the voice ordered.

"What?" said Trevor as he turned to see the newcomer.

"I said, give it back." Michael Halsey stood all alone at the edge of the court.

"Who's gonna make me?"

"I am," Michael said and held his breath.

The children watching gasped. No one saw that Michael was shaking.

Trevor looked around: none of the other children were going over to stand beside Michael. Good. Without support, Michael didn't stand a chance. Trevor was bigger, and he wasn't afraid to fight, so long as it was one-on-one and he was the bigger one.

Michael walked slowly, resolutely, across the court. He tried to swallow, but his mouth had gone dry. When he reached Trevor, he tried to sound commanding and fearless, but his words came out as barely more than a whisper, "It's not yours. Give it back."

Trevor let out a loud, "Ha!" and punched Michael in the face.

Michael fell to the ground — his eye screaming with pain.

Trevor turned and headed back toward the school, arms raised in victory. The other students moved to give him room to pass.

Benjamin walked over to Michael, "Thanks."

"For what?" Michael snapped, feeling like he'd just made a fool out of himself.

"For trying," said Benjamin as he reached down to help Michael up.

Beneath the branches of the distant western hemlock, Morgan watched the children disperse. She saw the victim come to the aid of his fallen defender. Morgan's eyes narrowed: there was something familiar about that boy — the one that had stood up and been knocked down. The aura of courage and leadership was unmistakable. She'd sensed it once before . . . in Camelot.

6

Michael walked into the empty science lab, sat down at his desk, crossed his arms, and glared at Mr. M.

John Merlin did not look up from his work. He was hanging up numerous posters of frogs — internal organs and all. "What happened to your eye?"

"I got some bad advice," Michael grumbled.

"Oh." Merlin went to the shelves at the side of the room and started to pour a strange, bubbling liquid into a large flask. "And what would have been 'good advice'?" he asked.

Michael looked away, "To mind my own business."

"But it was your business. It was everyone's business." Merlin shook the flask; it bubbled profusely.

"I don't see how," countered Michael, scowling.

"If you see that something's wrong, it's your responsibility to fix it."

"Who says?"

"I say."

Michael turned back to his teacher, "If everybody did that . . ." he paused to think.

Merlin noted the pause and smiled.

Michael looked at the floor, "Yeah, well, I'd still like to give Trevor a taste of his own medicine."

Merlin carried the flask with the bubbling liquid over to Michael's desk. "If something's wrong," he repeated gently, "then it's wrong." He held out the flask, "Here. Drink this."

Michael looked up, glad to change the subject, "What is it?"

Merlin shrugged, "A mysterious bubbling liquid."

Michael took the flask and sniffed. Cautiously, he took a sip, "It tastes like soda water."

"It is soda water," Merlin said and returned to the boxes at the front of the room. "Violence is always upsetting to the stomach."

Selena Sanchez was in her office reading through the morning's announcements when there was a knock on her door. "Come in," she called and looked up to greet her visitor. The first bell of the day shrieked a warning as the door opened to reveal a beautiful woman in a red dress.

Merlin's students were seated in a circle in the centre of the room. All of the desks had been pushed back toward the walls. In the middle of the circle was a large poster depicting the respiratory system of a frog. Merlin gave a stack of papers to Cory and asked him to take one and pass the rest along. Each page displayed a picture of a frog's respiratory system with blanks for the correct terms.

"Cool," said P.J. as she got her paper.

"Gross," said Tiffany.

"It's neither; it's just a piece of paper," Merlin's calm, steady voice infiltrated the conversation. He held up a large plastic model of a frog — the kind where the body parts go together like a puzzle. He passed it to Cory who instantly popped the eyeballs out. Merlin ignored the eyeballs as they bounced across the floor. "When you get the frog, take a close look at the heart and the lungs. Imagine them working together as part of a system." Merlin paused to allow for giggles as the frog's plastic intestines fell out.

"Breathing is part of the miracle of life —" Merlin stopped short. There was nothing miraculous about the plastic frog. It wasn't alive and it certainly wasn't breathing.

"All right. That's it," Merlin said as he suddenly stood up. The students stopped giggling. P.J. hid the frog's tongue under her hand and looked up at Mr. M.

Merlin pointed at the plastic frog, "This is not a frog. This is a piece of plastic. It does not have a respiratory system or a circulatory system. It just has more plastic." Merlin turned and grabbed a few of the extra posters from his desk. He tucked them under his arm and headed for the door, "Come on, everyone. Line up. Don't forget your paper and a pencil."

Excitement spread through the class. The plastic frog lay forgotten as each student scrambled to pick up their diagram sheet.

Merlin lead his class down the north stairway toward the exit farthest from the main office. He wasn't intending to leave the school property — but he didn't want to take any chances on Ms. Sanchez cancelling his "outing".

The finger-like tip of Glen Lake pointed directly onto the school's property. Merlin chose a spot along the tree-sheltered eastern' shore where he and his students could search for Pacific Tree Frogs. The day was mild, there was a slight breeze coming off the water, and the frog hunt turned out to be very successful.

Merlin called his class into a circle and sat down with one of the tiny frogs in his hands, as did many of the students. Tiffany spread out the posters in the centre of the circle.

Once they were settled. Merlin directed his students to close their eyes. As soon as everyone was quiet, Merlin began his rhythmic recitation, "Concentrate. See with your mind. See with your fingers. Gently now, remember a frog doesn't have any ribs. Feel the blood flowing to the heart. A frog's heart has only three chambers. Feel the deoxygenated blood being pumped to the lungs and the skin. A frog can take in air through its lungs, its skin and the roof of its mouth. Feel the oxygenated blood being pumped back through the body."

Merlin paused, "Now concentrate on your own heart. The human heart has four chambers. Feel your own blood entering the two chambers on the right side. Feel it being pumped to your lungs. Use your imagination: see the oxygen molecules, watch them being absorbed by your blood cells, see them turning bright red . . . watch them flowing back to your heart — being pumped through your body in an endless circle . . . the same endless circle that's flowing inside of the frog you're holding."

Some students rubbed their thumbs up and down the amphibians' bellies. Others used their fingers to trace delicate paths along the tiny creatures' extremities. The frogs did not struggle; it was almost as if they too were being carried away on the deep, even waves of Merlin's voice.

"Oh, no!" exclaimed Selena Sanchez as she stood, hands on her hips, in the open doorway of Merlin's science lab.

Morgan Le Fay looked around the empty classroom unable to see what was upsetting the principal.

"I'm sorry," explained Ms. Sanchez, "but they've disappeared — again!"

Morgan's eyes went wide, "disappeared?" she thought. "How many?" she asked.

"Thirty, all thirty," fumed Ms. Sanchez. "No permission, no note, nothing!"

Morgan stood in awe of Merlin's talent. He was able to make thirty people disappear. And it wasn't the first time!

She studied the room intently, looking for clues to Merlin's power. She saw the shelves packed with powders and liquids; she saw the pictures of frogs — inside and out. She saw the green frog model lying on the floor with its guts hanging out. Morgan could do a lot with a frog, but she'd never thought of turning one inside out. Merlin must be planning something incredible. She would have to be careful.

7

The little frog in John Merlin's hand struggled frantically to get free. He stroked it gently to calm it, but his palms were sweating. The feeling of foreboding had returned — stronger than ever. Merlin lost his grip on the now agitated frog just as he was saying, "Nature has much to teach us —"

Michael Halsey gestured to the frog as it hopped away, "Yeah, like 'escape the first chance you get!'"

The other students laughed and released their frogs. The children screamed and giggled as the amphibians jumped every-which-way in their rush to get back to the protective bushes along the lake's edge.

Merlin was trying to call his class back to order when a rustling in the bushes startled him. He turned and saw two women. The first was Principal Sanchez, furious; the second was the most beautiful woman he'd ever seen.

Morgan Le Fay smiled. She had no fear of being recognized, but she sensed his agitation and quickly spun a cloaking web around her thoughts to hide her intent.

Ms. Sanchez introduced her as a prospective parent — which Morgan quickly amended to "aunt". Morgan explained that she was inquiring on behalf of a nephew who was coming to stay with her.

"I'm sure your nephew will enjoy this school," Merlin began, "Miss . . .?"

"Please, call me Morgan."

Merlin stole a glance at his glowering principal and quickly added, "We have all the latest facilities."

"So I've seen," Morgan said, moving closer to him: she was trying to sense his power, gage his abilities.

The closer Morgan got, the more nervous Merlin seemed. She checked her cloaking web. It was intact. A slow smile spread across her dark red lips: he was attracted to her. She almost laughed out loud. She'd always suspected it, but the old fool had been adept at hiding his feelings. But this was a young fool, and he'd already made his first mistake: he'd bought her story without even holding up a simple truth mirror.

Ms. Sanchez excused herself and herded the children back toward the school. She checked her watch. They'd have to hurry if they were going to beat the second-period bell. Behind them, Merlin started to collect his diagrams — under the watchful eye of his visitor.

Morgan picked up a forgotten pencil. She turned it over in her hand, examining it closely. She knew the best way to discover something's strength was to test it.   Morgan waited until the departing principal had rounded the corner of the building — then she snapped the pencil in half.

- - -

Ms. Sanchez let out a scream as the shin bone of her right leg suddenly broke in half. She stumbled and fell to the ground.

"Now, Merlin," Morgan thought, "we will see how strong you really are." Morgan raised her hand to her necklace. "Snap and break, too brittle to bend," her voice was raspy and dry.

- - -

Ms. Sanchez looked at her impossibly crooked limb, but could see no outward signs of injury. She didn't know what was happening. Maybe she'd tripped and broken her leg. The students were crowding around her, trying to see what was wrong, trying to help. Michael ran to get the school nurse. Tiffany gently cradled Ms. Sanchez head in her lap. One of the other girls covered Ms. Sanchez with her sweater, the way they'd been taught in "emergency first aid".

Ms. Sanchez' other leg and both of her arms started to jerk violently. Tiffany screamed as she heard the awful cracking sounds. Ms. Sanchez fainted as six more of her bones broke.

- - -

"Is that a poem?" Merlin interrupted as he secured a rubber band around his posters.

Morgan concentrated on the memory of the principal; she could feel the woman's shock. Seven bones broken. No blood. She smiled, proud of the tidy little bit of magic.

"It has such a nice 'click-clacking' sound to it," Merlin commented as he came up beside Morgan.

She looked at him, not understanding.

"Your poem," Merlin prompted, "it reminds me of knitting needles — clicking and clacking together. Yes, busy knitting needles in loving hands," Merlin mused to himself, "making something warm and comforting — something strong and sure."

Morgan stared at him. He'd said the words so simply — as if they'd cost him no effort at all. She looked toward the school; she could sense the woman's bones mending, her fear retreating.

Morgan examined Merlin closely. His attitude toward her hadn't changed. Was it possible that he couldn't sense the origin of the magic?

"Tell me, uh, Morgan, what do you do for a living? Are you a poet? I always enjoy knowing a little bit about my students' parents — uh, aunts." Merlin smiled, hoping to draw Morgan's attention away from the distant school and back to himself. She was very beautiful, and he felt more than a little attracted to her. He was desperately trying to think of a way to ask her for a date that wouldn't make him look too foolish.

Morgan gazed into his eyes, trying to sense his strength, measure it. But he was like a blank wall. His cloaking web was far superior to hers — it was almost as if he hadn't realized he'd used any magic at all. And he kept smiling at her. It was very unnerving.

Tiffany saw the school's nurse running toward them. She looked down to check on Ms. Sanchez and was startled to see that her limbs were perfectly straight and she was sleeping peacefully.

Morgan Le Fay started to walk toward the school. John Merlin was instantly at her side, chatting, disrupting her concentration.

Everything would be all right, Morgan told herself — she just needed a more accurate gage of Merlin's power. She didn't want to risk zapping him and getting fried in the bargain.

To divert him, Morgan asked Merlin a few questions about frogs. As she listened to his detailed answer, she realized: words! He was good with words!

Morgan looked around as she walked, searching for an idea, a catalyst for her mental energy. She saw it and froze. Merlin nearly bumped into her.

Morgan looked at the tree, looked into the maze of its branches, saw the nest and spied the egg. She gave it a nudge with her mind and the delicate oval fell to the ground with a sickening "crack".

Ms. Sanchez felt something warm trickle down her forehead. Tiffany screamed.

Merlin dropped his posters and grabbed his head — searing pain sliced through his skull.

Morgan Le Fay looked at him and asked courteously, "Something wrong?"

"My head . . . hurts," Merlin managed to say.

The children closest to Tiffany and Ms. Sanchez panicked; some ran away; a few started to cry.

The nurse, in a commanding voice, ordered three of the students to run and tell the secretary to call 911. Then she turned her attention to the mysterious wound that had suddenly appeared on Ms. Sanchez's head.

"Can I get you anything?" Morgan offered.

"No . . . thank you . . . I . . ." Merlin took a couple of steps and sank to his knees. His head ached like someone had dropped it from a great height. He was overcome with the irrational fear that if he let go of his head, his brain would fall out.

Morgan was satisfied. She could sense that the woman's cracked skull was staying cracked. No bones were knitting now; no torn blood vessels sealing; no flesh healing. Merlin could be beaten.

She would need time to plan her attack just right. About eight hours ought to do it. Morgan helped Merlin to his feet. "I have to be going," she cooed in delicious tones, "but I'd like to continue our talk later — for my nephew's sake, of course."

"Later . . ." Merlin mumbled.

"Perhaps tonight," she whispered in his ear, "Dinner?"

Merlin kept his hands firmly pressed against the sides of his head. "Dinner?" he asked, not sure he'd heard her correctly.

"At your place."

"Uh . . . sure . . ." Merlin managed, unable to follow the conversation.

Morgan turned and headed toward the school, leaving Merlin to stumble along on his own.

She practically skipped the whole way.

She smiled as she rounded the corner. Such a pretty sight: the crowd of terrified people — the ambulance — the woman on the stretcher.

By the time Merlin reached the tarmac, the ambulance had left, and the teachers had gotten the rest of the students under control and back to class.

The nurse hurried over to him. "I'm sorry, in all the commotion I didn't see you. Mr. Carter has your class. I've called Ms. Sanchez' family. They're meeting the ambulance at Victoria General Hospital — " She suddenly noticed that Merlin was holding his head, "Are you all right, Mr. Merlin?"

Merlin tentatively lifted his hands a few centimetres away from his head. He held his breath. Nothing happened. His brain did not splatter onto the floor. He sighed and let his tired arms fall to his sides. His headache was going away.

He looked up and saw the nurse's strange expression, "I'm sorry," he said, "did you say something?" Only then did he notice her dress was spattered with blood.

Michael Halsey rode his bike home the long way. He was already late, but he didn't care. He couldn't get the day's events out of his mind. He kept seeing the principal lying on the ground; and he knew his mother was going to be mad when she saw his black eye.

Michael kept adding streets to his circuitous route, trying to pedal away his fear and frustration. He stopped for a red light in an unfamiliar neighborhood and froze.

The light changed, but Michael didn't move: down the street to his right was a sight that made the whole day worth living.

Michael watched as a group of much bigger, much older boys moved in on a lone target: Trevor.

With his back against a boarded-up storefront and no way out, Trevor watched his enemies approach. "Back off, Gordo, it's mine. I worked for it and I'm not givin' it up without a fight," Trevor bellowed, his legs straddling his fallen bike, his feet buried in spilled newspapers.

"Oh, you gonna fight all of us?" asked Gordon Leach, a ninth grader from Our Lady of Mercy.

"Why? You too chicken to face me alone?" countered Trevor, trying to sound tough.

"I don't get my hands dirty on small fry." Gordon gestured for his friends to move in on Trevor.

Trevor knew they meant business; his ribs still hurt from his last pay day. He shoved his hand into his pocket and gripped his money in a rock-hard fist. He didn't know how else to hang onto it. It wasn't the impending beating that upset him, it was going home empty-handed. The thought of his mother hugging him and saying it didn't matter almost made him cry, "Please, Gordo, I can't give it to you. My mom needs the money —"

"Like I don't?" Gordon said. He was about to add, "Get him!" when he was interrupted by a small, unfamiliar voice.

"Leave him alone."

Gordon and the others turned around to see a small black boy on a bicycle about fifteen metres away.

Trevor couldn't believe it. He looked around. Everyone's attention was on Michael. This was his chance to get away. He didn't move.

"I said, leave him alone." Michael was terrified.

"Who's gonna make me?"

"I am." Michael's voice was little more than a squeak.

"You?" Gordon laughed. "You and what army?" He gestured for the largest of his friends to advance on Michael.

"My brother's in a gang. If you don't leave us alone, they'll get you!" Michael blurted out his bluff then held his breath.

Gordon raised his hand in an "all stop" signal. He stared at Michael, trying to judge the situation. He hadn't heard of any gangs in or around Glen Lake, but he'd certainly heard about them on the mainland and south of the border.

Michael just sat there on his bike like he wasn't even scared.

Gordon decided that Michael was acting just cocky enough to be telling the truth. "Okay, we're outa here. But you tell your brother to keep away from us or he'll be sorry!"

Michael said nothing.

Gordon and his four thugs grabbed their skateboards and raced away.

Trevor picked up his newspapers, shoved them back in his delivery bag, and righted his bike. He walked it over to Michael. "Your brother really in a gang?" Trevor asked.

"My brother is three years old," Michael answered in a surly voice — he was still angry about this morning.

Trevor started to fidget. He wanted to say something like "thank you" or "I'm sorry," but he didn't know how. Instead, he just asked, "Why?"

Michael answered curtly, "If something's wrong — it's wrong."

Trevor looked Michael straight in the eye — he understood.

9

After school, John Merlin drove to Victoria General Hospital to visit Ms. Sanchez. He was stopped at the main desk — only family members were allowed to see her. Merlin explained he was a teacher at Ms. Sanchez's school and asked about her condition. The nurse on duty was happy to tell him that after sixty stitches and two dozen metal staples, Ms. Sanchez was in stable condition.

Stable condition: to Merlin, that didn't sound good enough. The nurse added that after further evaluation, Ms. Sanchez would probably be admitted to one of the brain injury rehabilitation programs at Gorge Road Hospital. Merlin thanked the nurse and decided to wait. He took a seat in the waiting room and stared at the clock. He looked through the pile of magazines but found nothing to interest him. Stable condition: no — not nearly good enough.

At the desk, the duty nurse whispered something to a man in green surgical garb; she pointed at Merlin.

The surgeon came over and introduced himself, "Excuse me, Kate says you teach at Glen Lake. I'm Doctor Halverson, one of the surgeons who — "

Merlin jumped up, "How is she?"

"She's very lucky. There's no trauma to the brain. In fact, there's no bruising whatsoever — very strange. Did you see the accident?"

"No, I just felt it."

"I beg your pardon?"

"No. I didn't see it," Merlin amended, "I was too far away. Was it very bad?"

"Yes and no. The bone plate is cracked in three places. That can produce a lot of scar tissue, which may cause epilepsy. But the brain itself is undamaged — like cracking an egg but not breaking the yolk. It's almost like something was holding the brain in place, protecting it. As I said, she's very lucky. I don't think we'll have to transfer her to Gorge Road after all."

"Oh," Merlin mumbled; he hadn't heard anything the doctor had said after the word "epilepsy".

"Why don't you go home and get some rest," Dr. Halverson suggested as he turned to leave. "You look tired."

Merlin nodded his thanks and sat back down on the couch. He had no intention of going home. He closed his eyes and tried to get comfortable. It was no use. Somewhere at the edge of his consciousness, a prickly kind of nagging kept him awake. Merlin had the annoying feeling that he was forgetting something.

Morgan Le Fay stood on the front step of Merlin's house, waiting. She looked at the setting sun sure that "dinner" time must be soon. She had spent the day preparing for this meeting. She touched her necklace; the magic was ready. She would waste no time on words. Merlin would never hear it coming.

In the hospital gift shop, Merlin looked for something to keep him busy while he waited. He looked through the selection of paperbacks, the rows of magazines, the stacks of crossword puzzles, then he saw it: a basket full of knitting needles and yarn.

Morgan Le Fay had let herself into Merlin's house and was sitting in the library surrounded by candles. She'd given up on him hours ago and was now methodically going through his books.

Merlin sat in the waiting room knitting happily. He'd chosen a ball of pink angora wool, and the soft fibre felt soothing in his fingers. The click-clack of his knitting needles echoed through the waiting room and down the hall — all the way to Ms. Sanchez's room.

10

It was seven a.m. and Dr. Halverson had finished his early rounds. He'd ordered a C.A.T. scan of his patient and was looking at the film. His forehead furrowed. "There must be some mistake," he said to the technician.

"No, I double checked." The technician had been waiting for the doctor's response.

Dr. Halverson held up the film to emphasize his point, "But this cranium is normal, no cracks!"

"Yeah, but look," the technician took the film and held it up to the light, "you can still see the staples we put in."

Up on the third floor, Merlin awoke to the last face he expected to see. Staring down at him was Selena Sanchez. "Mr. Merlin, have you been here all night?"

Merlin sat up and tried to straighten his hair, his tie. "Uh, yes . . . I must have fallen asleep," he answered, distracted. He was trying to remember the pieces of a dream he'd been having.

Ms. Sanchez was sitting in a wheel chair. She was wearing a bathrobe over her hospital gown and her head was wrapped in bandages. "Well, now I don't know what to think." she said.

"I'm sorry, I don't —" Merlin began.

"I was feeling so good this morning, I decided to call the school. Dinah said she tried to reach you to tell you to take the day off. A Child Psychologist is coming to spend the day with your class; yesterday was very upsetting for everyone."

"Oh, that's a good idea—"

"As I was saying, when she couldn't reach you by phone, she asked Mr. Carter to stop by your house on his way in, and who do you think he found there?"

"Who?" asked Merlin.

"Miss Le Fay — the parent I introduced you to yesterday on your 'field trip'."

Merlin shook his head; he'd only been half listening. The dream was coming back to him. Something about knitting needles and holding a brain in his hands. "Wait a minute," Merlin interrupted, "shouldn't you be in bed?"

"Yes, but I feel just fine. I know this looks bad," she said, gesturing to the bandages around her head, "but I feel great."

Merlin stared. Ms. Sanchez really did look like she was feeling better. He tried to focus his attention on something she had just said. Something important.

Ms. Sanchez nodded toward a small pink bundle that had fallen to the floor. "What's that?"

Merlin picked up his creation and held it out to her, "I made this for you."

Ms. Sanchez took the gift. When she saw what Merlin had made, tears came to her eyes. It was a little pink hat. The stress of the last twenty-four hours came flooding over her, "They had to shave my head, you know," she said with an uncharacteristic quiver. "Thank you."

Merlin watched as Ms. Sanchez gently stroked the soft angora wool. As he stared, something clicked. In a flash he knew that everything was going to be all right. He knew the cracked bone plate of her cranium was already mending — had been mending all night. Mending while Merlin had been knitting.

Merlin froze. An image of bones knitting while needles knitted hung before him.

A nurse came over to them with a kind reminder to Ms. Sanchez that she shouldn't "over do it". Ms. Sanchez nodded, said good-bye to Merlin, and let the nurse wheel her back to her room.

Merlin stared after her, coming to an impossible conclusion. Almost as if the realization had stung him, Merlin jumped off the couch, ran down the hall, caught the elevator to the lobby and headed for the main exit. He had to tell someone.

11

Morgan Le Fay stared at her own name in print. She had been going through Merlin's books when she'd come across the first inkling of the nightmare that stared back at her from the page.

Morgan had found a book called "The Hollow Hills" by T.H. White. She'd started searching it for Merlin's possible hiding places when she saw his name. She flipped pages; again and again she found his name. Then on one page she saw "Arthur". Impossible. This book documented Arthur's tutelage by Merlin. Impossible. It hadn't happened yet.

She scoured the other books. Again and again she found them, "Merlin" and "Arthur". She found them in poetry, in short stories, in novels. And every now and then she'd find herself. Some of the accounts were wildly inaccurate, others dangerously close to the truth.

And the pictures — she'd been depicted with every hair and eye colour possible, every style and feature available. But always beautiful — Morgan consoled herself with that. She closed the book.

Something had gone very wrong.

Morgan meticulously went over the magic she'd used to get here. She checked every nuance of her memory for the error that could have caused such a profound deviation.

She had traveled through time to Merlin's youth. She was sure of that.

First, she thought she might have found the wrong Merlin, but after considering yesterday's little exhibition, she was sure she had the right magician.

So, if Merlin was the right Merlin, and he was young — the error lay in time. She'd traveled to the wrong time. Merlin must have managed to compromise her magic in some way.

This was the future — not the past — Morgan reasoned. Otherwise, she wouldn't be able to read so many accounts of Arthur's life. But a future in which the Romans had returned to Briton — what other explanation could there be for the amazing inventions, the incredible condition of the roads?

Before Arthur's death, in the lands not under his protection, the roads had already started to disappear: their stones having been stolen by peasants and invaders alike to build their houses. Morgan rubbed her forehead; why hadn't she seen it before? The abundance of food all around her attested to the return of the light, maneuverable Roman plow. But she still didn't have her finger on the whole of the problem; something eluded her. If she and the young Merlin had been swept into the wrong time, then he would be as new to it as she was. He couldn't be so entrenched as to have a job, a house, and neighbors who knew him well enough to worry about his garbage.

Morgan took a deep breath to calm herself. She'd made a mistake — she was sure of that now. But how big of a mistake? The first thing she had to do was find out the date.

Dr. Cassandra Westinghouse shared her chicken-salad sandwich with John Merlin. She'd had a cancellation and was enjoying an early lunch when Merlin popped in with his news.

"And your principal is really going to be all right?" Cassandra asked.

"Yes, I believe so. I know this is going to sound crazy, but I think I'm responsible."

"John, when there's a tragedy, especially one involving a close friend or colleague, people often feel responsible, even when it wasn't their fault. You can't blame yourself."

"No, no, you don't understand. I'm responsible for her recovery, for her bones knitting, for her brain not getting bruised."

Dr. Westinghouse put down her sandwich, "Now, John, you know that's not possible."

"I know, but it is. I knew it this morning — when I saw Ms. Sanchez stroking the hat I had knitted. How else do you explain her prognosis? Don't you get it? I wanted her to get better and she did. My knitting, my desire — together they had power." Merlin dropped his voice to a whisper, "Magic."

Cassandra's voice was very calm; she made an effort to speak slowly, "You're telling me that you healed Ms. Sanchez with magic?"

"Yes."

"John —"

"Merlin."

Cassandra raised her eyebrows.

"Merlin, it's my name."

Dr. Cassandra Westinghouse scrutinized her patient: his clothes were wrinkled; he was unshaven; his eyes were red from lack of sleep. But there was something more, something deeper — a confidence that lit him up from the inside, an exuberance that his fatigue couldn't dampen. He seemed — despite his appearance, and for lack of a better word — powerful.

Cassandra had seen such confidence before in some of the patients she'd worked with at the Institute. It denoted a mania that she knew would be followed by a terrible and crushing low. But John Merlin was not suffering from manic depression. He was obsessed with discovering his identity, his roots, his past. Many people who were adopted shared that passion. Dr. Westinghouse discretely turned on her tape recorder.

Fifteen hundred years. Almost fifteen hundred years! Morgan Le Fay sat down on the curb beside the newspaper box. Fifteen hundred years -- how could Merlin's feeble meddling have caused her to make a mistake so enormous? How could Arthur still be remembered after all this time?

Morgan looked down at her feet. A small black puddle of oil lay glittering in the late morning sun. Its surface was smooth and dark and shiny — like obsidian. Morgan waved her hand across the puddle and watched as tiny tongues of light arced across its oily surface. Merlin's candles. They were still there, glowing well into the future — a future beyond even this one.

Morgan whispered a hypothesis and looked to see what would happen if she kept to her original plan and killed Merlin.

The bottom half of the arc disappeared. Morgan wasn't sure what it meant. Maybe the memory of past achievements would be lost. But the future was so bright. Merlin must have already lit a candle.

But who? Whose life would be so inspirational that it would light up the future?

Morgan paused then smiled. She'd already seen him: the boy who had reminded her of Camelot. The boy who was already Merlin's student.

Morgan looked back at the puddle, this time with the hypothesis that the boy would cease to exist.

The top half of the arc sputtered and went dark.

Fine. She'd just have to kill them both.

Dr. Westinghouse listened as Merlin told her everything: the frogs, the field trip, the visit from Ms. Sanchez and Morgan. Merlin paused — there was something he was forgetting, something from this morning, something lost in the excitement of his self-discovery, something about Morgan. He told Cassandra about Morgan staying behind to help him with his posters and then agreeing to see him later that evening — which, in the confusion, he'd forgotten all about.

Merlin went into great detail about Morgan's poetry, about his migraine, about the feeling that his brain was going to fall out. "You see, if Morgan hadn't recited that poem with its brittle words, I never would have thought about the sound knitting needles make. I guess you could say, without her help, I never would have discovered my true identity. Ms. Sanchez said Mr. Carter saw her at my house this morning. I hope she's not too mad about being stood-up —" Merlin froze. The colour drained from his face.

"What is it?" Cassandra asked.

"Morgan," Merlin said the name slowly, as if he were hearing it for the first time. "This morning, at the hospital, Ms. Sanchez called her 'Miss Le Fay' —"

"Le Fay?" Cassandra asked then paused, "As in 'Morgan Le Fay'?"

Merlin nodded, "I didn't put it together until just now."

Cassandra's eyes narrowed. "Are you trying to tell me that a woman named Morgan Le Fay helped you realize you were Merlin the Magician?" She clenched her jaw. She was being had. "This has gone on long enough," Cassandra said through her teeth. "I understand that yesterday was traumatic for you, and that you've been under some stress lately, and that you sometimes feel lonely and lost and unconnected. I know you want to know your family; I know you want a deeper understanding of who you are. But really! Is it because you don't think I'm helping you as fully as I can — as fast as you want?"

"Oh, no!" Merlin shot out of his chair, "She was in my house!" He ran for the door.

Cassandra didn't believe a word of Merlin's story. But she could see something was deeply and desperately wrong. She made her decision in an instant, grabbed her purse, scribbled a note for her secretary, and ran after her patient.

12

Morgan Le Fay stood in the playground looking up at the school. Should she wait for them to come out or should she go in after them? Morgan's eyes narrowed — she was tired of waiting.

Michael Halsey sat fidgeting at the back of the science lab. At the front of the room, a young therapist was talking about the time she saw a car accident. Michael squirmed in his seat. He was starting to feel strange, uncomfortable — like he was in the wrong place; like he was too hot, or too cold; like he wanted a drink, or needed some fresh air. The feeling was overwhelming. He had to get out of the classroom — he didn't know why; he just had to get out. Michael raised his hand and asked to go to the bathroom.

Practically dancing up the south stairway, humming a curse, came Morgan Le Fay. In a few minutes, all would be darkness.

Michael walked toward the boys' bathroom but didn't go in. Instead, he quietly slipped down the north stairs.

Morgan was the epitome of confidence as she reached the second floor landing. She practically floated down the hall to Merlin's classroom. But as she peered in through the open door, her smile faded. Neither Michael nor Merlin was in the room. Instead, a young woman was asking the students to share their feelings.

Morgan stepped back into the shadow of a doorway and closed her eyes, extending her senses. She couldn't feel Merlin; his cloaking web was very strong. But she was surprised to find that she couldn't feel the boy either. Could Merlin's web be so powerful as to hide them both? No matter. Morgan knew where the shrine of lists was kept; all she needed now was one little piece of information.

In the main office, Morgan Le Fay stood playing with her necklace. She described a boy to the secretary: thin frame, eager eyes, short hair, beautiful ebony skin. It was only after Morgan added the ingredient of Merlin's science class that the secretary's blank expression lit up with recognition. "Michael Halsey," she announced, as if expecting a prize.

13

John Merlin and Dr. Cassandra Westinghouse pulled into Merlin's driveway. Merlin turned off the engine but didn't take off his seat belt. He just sat there staring at his house like he'd never seen it before.

Cassandra watched him closely. She started to say something but stopped, changed her mind, and asked instead, "What are you afraid of?"

Merlin looked directly at her, "I'm afraid that I'm not crazy."

Cassandra smiled, "You're not crazy."

With a burst of decision, Merlin unclipped his seat belt, jumped out of the car and bolted up his front steps.

The door was wide open. He froze on the threshold. Cassandra followed him up the steps and joined him in the doorway. Together they peered inside.

Merlin closed his eyes and stepped over the threshold. As soon as his foot touched the floor inside, he relaxed. The house was safe. He could feel it. Morgan Le Fay had left no trap, set no ambush.

Cassandra followed him inside; she could see the change in him immediately. His attitude became purposeful; he began systematically searching through his house.

Merlin didn't know what he was looking for, so he was terribly afraid he would miss it — something that would prove he really was Merlin the Magician — something that would prove Morgan Le Fay really was his evil nemesis. Something that would finally give him an identity — however implausible.

The living room and kitchen were just as he had left them two days ago. The bedroom was unchanged. Merlin was beginning to doubt himself. He looked at Dr. Westinghouse and saw that she was watching his every move, her concern deepening with every passing minute.

Merlin stepped into the library. Candles of every description had been placed all around the room. Their stems were short and their wicks were black: they'd burned for some time before being snuffed out. Inspired, Merlin looked at the light switch. It was set in the off position. He reached for it and flipped it upward. The two reading lamps came on instantly.

"Look!" Merlin called. Cassandra stepped into the room and looked at the lights. Merlin pointed to the candles as if somehow that would explain everything. "Don't you see?" Merlin said, both eyebrows raised as if waiting for a difficult answer from a new student.

"See what?"

"The light switch. It was set to off. But the lights work." Merlin waited, both eyebrows disappearing into his hairline.

Cassandra was not in the habit of providing answers for her patients.

"There's no need for candles," Merlin answered for her, "unless you don't know what a light switch is for! Morgan Le Fay wouldn't know about light switches."

Cassandra's eyes narrowed. This was no longer a woman named Morgan Le Fay — John was accepting her as the genuine article. "Let's go back to my office."

"And how did she light the candles?" Merlin asked. "Do you see any spent matches?" He lowered his voice to a whisper, "Magic!"

Cassandra's voice was flat, "Or maybe she had a lighter in her purse."

Three. There were three "Halseys" in the book of lists. None of them "Michael". Morgan Le Fay was unruffled; she assumed the book simply listed the name of the most significant adult per location. In this case: probably dear little Michael's father. All she had to do was pick the right one. She memorized the three addresses and set off in search of the first one.

Merlin and Dr. Westinghouse stood in the library. Cassandra was speaking quietly, "Many people feel bound to live up to their names: Rockefeller, Barrymore, Lennon, Kennedy . . ."

"Um hm," Merlin intoned, not really listening. Something was bothering him.

"John, you already are someone special," Cassandra continued. "You have degrees in Chemistry and Physics. You're a respected teacher. Identifying with Merlin the Magician is . . . unnecessary. John?"

Merlin's eyes opened wide. He spun around and stared at his bookcase. There was a big hole in it.

"Merlin," Cassandra continued, she was using her firm voice now, "is a fictional character, as is Morgan Le Fay. You cannot decide to become a fictional character to avoid the real world — no matter how much it may have scared you yesterday. No matter how worried you are about your principal."

"Merlin isn't fictional, neither's King Arthur, but I always thought that Morgan Le Fay was —" Merlin froze.

"Was what?"

"A thief! Look, this entire section of books is missing. All my books about Camelot. It took me years to collect them." Merlin's eyes narrowed, "She took them — but why?"

"That's enough. John, I want you to look at me. Look me in the eye and listen very carefully. You are not Merlin the Magician. A woman may have been here last night, but she is not an enchantress; I seriously doubt that her name is Morgan Le Fay, and there is no King Arthur."

"You're right."

"I'm right?"

"I don't have any students named Arthur." Merlin turned to the window, "It would have to be someone special," he thought out loud, "someone bright, someone full of potential." Merlin's voice dropped to a whisper, "Someone with enough courage to stand up for those weaker than himself."

Morgan Le Fay shifted her heavy purse to her other shoulder and walked away from the three-bedroom bungalow with the nice lawn and picket fence. The family inside was clearly of Saxon decent, not the deep, rich Abyssinian bloodline she was looking for.

14

Michael Halsey had ridden his bike around the mall parking lot for a while then gone over to the arcade. He was just about to buy a Popsicle when he got the strongest feeling that he should go home. Like that song people sing to ladybugs, his mind was full of images of fire and children all alone.

Michael got back on his bike and peddled as fast as he could. He came to a corner, saw the stop sign, ignored it, and veered to the right — practically running over a woman in a red dress. The woman jumped back, startled.

Michael fought to maintain control of his bike. Something told him that falling off, right here, right now, would be very bad.

Morgan Le Fay recognized Michael instantly. As she watched him struggle to bring the narrow two-wheeled chariot under control, her attention was drawn to the device. She looked closer and saw that a chain lead from a disc between Michael's feet to the hub of the rear wheel. Morgan smiled; this was no more than a simple two wheel pulley system. Without knowing its name, Morgan understood the contraption Michael was riding. For a moment, she forgot about destroying him and concentrated on his feet. They were turning a big pulley which sent the power from his legs to a smaller pulley on the rear wheel. The smaller pulley turned faster than Michael's legs — Morgan's eyes grew wide. With such a device, Michael could move fast. Very fast.   Michael could feel the woman's eyes all over him, all over his bike.

Morgan stared at the chain circling between the two pulleys. Its links were being grabbed and propelled by metal points jutting out from the discs like teeth in a gear. If one or more of the links should miss the teeth, the entire chain would go slack. It would become useless. The device would slow down — stop.

Morgan smiled. She touched her necklace and gave the chain a nudge with her mind.

Michael's feet began to spin. The pedals were moving but nothing was happening. His chain had come loose. Michael started to lose control of the bike. He weaved dangerously close to the gutter. Frantically, he kicked at his pedals, hoping to jar the chain back into place. It worked. Michael regained his balance, steered the bike back onto the road, and sped toward home.

Morgan realized that Michael was getting away, but she wasn't worried. She knew exactly where he was going. Thirty-three Cedar Drive was the last address on her list.

John Merlin's car was parked outside thirty-three Cedar Drive. He and Dr. Cassandra Westinghouse sat in the car looking at the pretty little house behind the row of western red cedars that lined the aptly named street.

"Are you satisfied?" Cassandra asked, "Look around. Everything is normal. Safe. The house hasn't been magicked out of existence or sucked into some vortex."

"Doctor, I'm not crazy. I know I sound crazy, but I'm not." Merlin had to look away from Dr. Westinghouse; the pity and worry in her eyes were too much for him to take.

Cassandra sighed, "We came to check on the house, like you wanted. Now we're going to check out the rest of your story, like I suggested."

"Please, I just want to warn his mother."

Cassandra shook her head, "And what are you going to say to her: 'Morgan Le Fay is out to get your son; I know because I'm Merlin the Magician'?"

Merlin looked hurt. Cassandra regretted her sarcastic tone, but she wasn't going to let him upset innocent people. Especially people who could make it difficult for him once this manifestation of emotional strain had passed.

Merlin wasn't about to give up, "I could just tell her to watch out for a woman in a red dress. A woman with long black hair, wearing a gold and silver snake necklace."

Cassandra opened the car door, "Slide over, I'm driving."

"But —"

"First, we're going to your school to check the name of yesterday's visitor. You might have misheard it. Second, we're going to the hospital to check on your principal's condition. Third, we're going back to my office and have a nice long talk. Finally, you're going home and getting a good night's sleep."

Merlin looked at Cassandra. She was seriously concerned and not about to listen to any more of his arguments. He decided to give in, for now. He could always make an inconspicuous phone call to Mrs. Halsey from the school or the hospital.

Cassandra got out of the car and walked around to the driver's side.

Merlin slid over to the passenger seat and looked out the window. He glanced at the tiny but well-kept lawns, at the toys in the driveways, at the mail carrier making his rounds.

As Merlin watched, the mail carrier walked up the path to the Halsey home and rang the bell. A moment passed then the door was opened by an attractive woman who was trying to dry a small child's hair while doing up buttons and giving kisses. Mrs. Cecelia Halsey signed for the package, thanked the carrier and took both it and the giggling child back inside.

As Cassandra opened the driver's door, she glanced into the side-view mirror and saw a figure in the distance. A woman in a red dress was heading in their direction.

Cassandra shook her head and climbed in beside Merlin. She turned the keys in the ignition and started the engine. As she pulled away from the curb, she checked the rear-view mirror and caught a flash of gold and silver from around the woman's neck.

Michael rode his bide up the alley behind his house. He opened the gate and slipped into his backyard. Good, his little brother wasn't playing outside. If his mom caught him skipping school, he'd be in big trouble. Michael looked up to his bedroom window. It would be quite a climb: the fence to the trellis to the tree to the window. He'd imagined doing it a hundred times.

At the school, Dr. Westinghouse flipped through the pages of the guest book. She ran her finger down the page with yesterday's date and stopped underneath a distinctive flowery script: Morgan Le Fay. There was no mistaking the name. She read it again then turned to look at Merlin. He was standing beside the telephone on the counter, nonchalantly tapping his fingers on the receiver.

Three-year-old William was dried and dressed. He sat on a kitchen chair swinging his legs and picking the raisins out of an oatmeal-raisin cookie. The doorbell rang. Mrs. Halsey looked up then back down at William. She eyed the raisins in his hand, "In your mouth or in the garbage."

William smiled and nodded, chewing bits of raisin-free oatmeal cookie. Mrs. Halsey went to answer the door. As soon as she was out of the kitchen, William scrambled to stand on his chair. He leaned over the kitchen table, reached for the sugar bowl and carefully buried each raisin in the soft white granules.

Mrs. Halsey straightened her blouse and opened the door. Standing on her threshold was a beautiful woman in a red dress. The woman's shiny black hair reached all the way down her back; around her neck she wore the most stunning necklace.

15

Upstairs, the floorboards creaked as Michael tiptoed to the stairs. He'd made it through the window and was creeping toward the landing. He bent down by the banister and listened. His mom was talking to someone at the front door, but he couldn't see who. Silently, he slid down a couple of steps and pressed his face between two of the banister's carved wooden posts.

"Yes?" Mrs. Halsey asked, expecting a sales pitch.

The woman in red spoke as if she were talking to an underling, "I am here to see Michael Halsey."

"I'm sorry, Michael's in school," Mrs. Halsey answered, suddenly cautious. "Who are you?"

"He is not at the school. I saw him outside only a few minutes ago."

Mrs. Halsey's eyes went wide: Michael skipping school! Her feelings of ill-ease were forgotten. "Thank you," she said to the woman and turned back into her home, calling, "Michael Alexander Halsey! If you're in this house you better come out right now, mister!"

William peered around the kitchen door, he knew that tone of voice and was glad it wasn't aimed at him. Maybe he should get the raisins out of the sugar, just in case.

Mrs. Halsey forgot all about the front door. She didn't see the woman step inside; she didn't hear the door snicker shut.

Michael cringed at the sound of disappointment in his mother's voice. She was more than angry; she was hurt. His first thought was to hide, but that never worked; his mother always found him. Instead, he gripped the banister posts and waited. His mother came through the downstairs archway and stood staring up at him with an expression of genuine surprise.

Michael was about to explain, about to beg for forgiveness, when he saw a woman come up behind his mother. He'd seen the woman before: the scarlet dress, the raven hair. She looked up at him. Their eyes met.

That was all it took and the magic was released.

Without thinking, Morgan had accidentally let loose the powerful attack she'd prepared for Merlin. Morgan cringed. She'd just wasted a great deal of work where simple strangulation would have sufficed.

Morgan stepped back and raised a protective shield around herself. The magical onslaught had been specifically designed to destroy a master magician, not a twelve-year-old boy. Simply put, it was too much magic for the target. There would be significant overkill.

John Merlin furtively dialed a number on the hospital's courtesy phone while Dr. Cassandra Westinghouse spoke to the duty nurse at the desk.

"So soon?" Cassandra asked, surprised. "I thought her injuries were more severe."

"So did we, at first," explained the nurse. "But her recuperative powers are phenomenal. Dr. Halverson intends to write her up in the medical journal."

"We have to go," Merlin interrupted hastily, taking hold of Cassandra's arm.

Cassandra turned and saw his frightened expression, "What is it?"

"I just called Michael's house. I couldn't get through."

"Maybe they went out —"

"No. I couldn't get through. The operator came on and said there was some trouble on the line. I asked her to try the number again but she said the problem was originating at the house. I've got a bad feeling . . ."

16

The walls started to smoke. Not the walls exactly, something inside them.

Morgan Le Fay's attack had been set to seek out magic and to consume the person wielding it. But there had been no magic in the house. Instead, the power she'd released had found the electricity, and mistaking it for magic, had attacked it.

The electricity, which had been flowing easily through the wires of the house, ready to branch off at the close of a circuit or the flip of a switch, suddenly met a magical force of resistance. The potential voltage of the electricity began to rise with the buildup of pressure as it tried to push its way through the magic.

The magic, beginning to understand its foe, pulled itself thin then wound itself in a constricting spiral around the electrical wiring running throughout the house.

The resistance was too much and the wires soon grew hot. Hot enough to melt their rubber shielding, hot enough to allow little electrical sparks to leak away into the dry insulation between the walls, setting it on fire.

The needle in the electrical meter on the outside of the Halsey's house began to spin, indicating the sudden surge of electricity that was being pulled into the home's electrical system. Fuses blew and breakers broke, but it was too late. The magic ran along the wires, forming little bridges and closing circuits. The electricity seemed to come alive. Almost as if it had been animated by the magic. It was fighting for its life.

Morgan smiled, safe behind her shield of protection.

The electrical fire-storm raged in the narrow space between the walls of Michael Halsey's home. Michael didn't notice. He was too busy looking in all directions at once. The house was bursting with light and sound. Every electrical light and appliance had suddenly come on. From the kitchen, William screamed. Mrs. Halsey turned and ran to her baby.

William stood in the middle of the kitchen, wailing. The broken sugar bowl lay at his feet. All around him, appliances whirred, blinked, danced and sputtered. The kettle boiled, the toaster popped, the blaring radio fell to the floor and burst into pieces and sparks. The electricity was trying to escape from the magic by transforming itself into heat, light, movement and sound. The microwave rocked off its stand, missing William's head by centimetres. He just stood there crying, too terrified to move, not knowing what to do.

Mrs. Halsey ran into the kitchen and froze. Bursts of flame crackled from the electric outlets. Tendrils of smoke swirled into the air. A strange electrical liquid seemed to be dripping down the walls — forming blue and silver puddles on the floor. The sputtering puddles of excited electrons were producing rivulets that flowed across the pink and white tile floor like currents in the tributary system of a powerful river. The tributaries were reaching for William.

In a heartbeat, Mrs. Halsey covered the distance between her and her youngest son. She scooped him up into her arms. William screamed louder. Mrs. Halsey tried to cover his ears with one arm while gripping him tightly with the other. Everything was happening at once. Fire, smoke, noise. She couldn't think.

Out. She had to get the children out. She looked back to the hallway and screamed, "Michael!" She couldn't see him.

She looked at the floor and saw that her path was cut off by flowing rivers of magically altered electricity. Mrs. Halsey had no idea what was happening or what she was seeing. "Michael!" she screamed again.

"Mom!"

She heard his voice. He was okay, for now. She couldn't get to him, not with William in her arms. Should she get William out and then come back for Michael? She had the strangest feeling that once she left the house she would never get back in.

The window. If she was careful, she could get William safely outside without actually leaving the house herself.

Afraid to step in the dangerous-looking liquid energy running all over her kitchen floor, Mrs. Halsey grabbed a wooden chair and climbed onto it. She struggled to maintain her hold on William who was now whimpering softly into her shoulder. She climbed from the chair onto the table and from the table onto the now empty microwave stand. It was hard to concentrate with the noise of the smoke detectors ringing in her ears and the frightening sight of her appliances banging against the counter or crashing to the floor. There was a hail of sparks as several electrical cords ripped free of the outlets. It was getting hard for Mrs. Halsey to breathe in the smoke, and William was getting heavy. She had to balance very carefully on the small stand.

As she struggled to get the window open, her motion sent the little wooden microwave cart rocking violently. Mrs. Halsey gripped the window frame to steady herself. William's arms were wrapped around her neck like a vice. The window was stuck. She looked around for something within reach to break it: nothing. Frantic, she started pounding on the glass.

John Merlin struggled with the passenger-side window of his car. It wouldn't open. He was having trouble breathing; he needed air! Beside him, Dr. Cassandra Westinghouse was saying something as she drove, but he couldn't hear her over the ringing in his ears.

Cassandra saw Merlin's distress and knew she should stop the car, but she had been overcome by a terrible foreboding. She told herself over and over that she'd gotten too involved in her patient's problem, that she was experiencing some form of physical empathy or transference or — she couldn't remember the right term — she couldn't think of anything — except getting back to the Halsey house. She stepped on the gas and broke the speed limit.

Merlin banged on the window, shouting in fury and frustration, "Open!"

Mrs. Halsey nearly fell off the microwave cart as the window suddenly opened wide. She caught herself, shifted her position so that William's back was toward the opening, and started to lift him out. William was having none of it. "Honey, baby, please. Mommy wants you to be outside."

"No!"

"Please baby, please. Mommy loves you, but the house is on fire. Remember we talked about fire? We said we have to go outside."

William wasn't listening. His eyes were closed tight, and he clung to his mother like a dead weight. Mrs. Halsey steeled herself and tore his little hands away from her neck.

"Mommy!" William screamed — his eyes wide with betrayal and fear.

"Oh, baby, baby, please. You wait for mommy outside. Mommy has to go get Michael."

William was screaming uncontrollably as Mrs. Halsey forced him through the window and lowered him as well as she could toward the little garden in back of the kitchen. Her heart broke as she pulled her hands free of his tiny grasp and let him fall gently to the soft earth below. She didn't have time to try to give him instructions like: go to the neighbor's house, or even, stay where you are. She doubted he would have heard her through his tears anyway.

William was out of the house; she would have to be content with that much for now. She turned back into the kitchen and looked toward the hall. She couldn't see Michael. She looked at the phone on the wall by the sink. She wanted to call 911, but sparks were exploding from the phone's mounting bracket and the strange liquid was running down the wall behind it.

Mrs. Halsey looked at the floor — it was a river of flowing electricity. Somewhere in her mind, she knew that didn't exactly make sense, but it was the closest thing she could think of to describe what she was seeing. What Mrs. Halsey didn't know was that Morgan's magic had become a liquid conductor for the ever-increasing multitude of electrons being pulled into the wiring system of her house.

Mrs. Halsey called out, "Michael!"

"Mom!" the response was immediate but faint, like Michael was having trouble getting enough air. Mrs. Halsey knew that in smoke they should be crawling on the floor, but the floor was no longer an option. Michael was on the stairs. She called out for him to move down to the lowest step. Then she looked around for a way to ford her kitchen.

Mrs. Halsey made the jump back to the kitchen table with surprising ease. Fear and adrenaline were great motivators. She stood on one kitchen chair, reached over and slid a second one in front of it. Mrs. Halsey watched as little electric splashes tried to climb up the wooden legs of the chairs. She knew that wood would insulate her from the electricity and planned to cross the floor by moving the chairs along as she jumped from one to the other. It was a good plan — and it worked — until she reached the archway.

Dr. Cassandra Westinghouse gripped the steering wheel as she drove; her hands were sweating. Beside her, John Merlin squirmed in his seat. He had managed to get the window open, but was now contorting himself into a variety of positions in an effort to keep his feet from touching the floor.

They were almost there. Cassandra had the strangest feeling: like she was watching herself from a distance. She knew she needed to take control of the situation, for everyone's sake, but her mind was full of smoke. She drove on, squinting as if trying to see through a dark cloud.

Mrs. Halsey could just make out Michael crouched at the bottom of the stairs. She slid the front chair into the hallway and stepped onto it, "Hold on sweetheart, I'm com —"

As she came into the hall proper, Mrs. Halsey gasped. Standing to her right was the woman who had come looking for Michael. She was surrounded by a funnel of wind that whipped her hair and dress into dizzying swirls. The woman's eyes were open and staring at Michael.

Morgan Le Fay watched the boy huddled in a ball at the base of the stairs. She was dimly aware of the mother, now in the hall. Just a little more time and the boy would succumb to the effects of the magical battle all around him.

17

Mrs. Halsey was a strong woman, but in her wildest dreams she had never imagined such a sight. She had been staring, transfixed, at the apparition in the red dress when it had smiled. The sight of the horrifying emotion crossing the beautifully evil face caused Mrs. Halsey to lose her grip on the chair. Fear closed around her heart, and she lost her balance.

Mrs. Halsey frantically grabbed for some support, but it was too late. She landed on her hands and knees in the shallow but sizzling electric sea. Little electric shocks instantly snapped at her wrists and knees, burning her flesh, but the mutated power did not explode inside of her. She was not the target the magic was looking for — she was not the ground the electricity needed to escape.

John Merlin's car screeched to a stop in front of the Halsey's house. Merlin and Dr. Westinghouse jumped out and ran for the front door. Merlin banged and shouted. Cassandra looked around for signs of trouble. The house looked normal, but from deep inside, she could hear the wail of smoke detectors, and from somewhere in the distance — the sound of a child crying.

Merlin stopped shouting, stopped banging. He became very quiet. Cassandra looked at him. Suddenly, his eyes opened wide and he screamed, "No!"

"What is it?" Cassandra asked, strangely afraid.

"We have to find another way in," Merlin said, stepping away from the locked front door. "Come on!" he yelled as he started to run around the side of the house. Cassandra followed, noting they were heading toward the sound of the crying.

Inside the house, Mrs. Halsey screamed. Morgan Le Fay didn't hear it; all her senses were tuned outward. Something was happening; someone was coming: Merlin!

Merlin and Cassandra rounded the back of the house and saw little William sitting in the garden, sobbing. Above him, acrid smoke billowed out of the open kitchen window. Within, crazy noises could be heard: little motors running, smoke alarms ringing.

Cassandra ran to William and scooped him up into her arms. She hugged him and told him everything would be all right. His eyes were wide, and he was gulping air. He'd cried so hard he was nearly hyperventilating. Cassandra looked at the open window. "I'm calling 911," she announced in a tone that precluded any arguments.

"I'm going in," Merlin announced in the exact same tone.

Cassandra didn't want to fight about it. She carried William a short distance into the backyard, away from the house. She sat down on the grass with him in her lap and dug in her purse for her cellular phone.

Merlin grabbed the sides of the window frame and started to hoist himself up. As soon as his feet were off the ground, his hold gave way. Actually, it disappeared. Merlin fell on his back in the garden. He stared up at the wall where the window had been.

Cassandra flipped open her phone and froze. She stared up at the house. All the windows were gone. Upstairs and down. The house was a brick cube.

Merlin looked at her, "I have to get in. She'll kill them — I know it." Merlin anxiously turned back to the solid brick wall facing him.

"I'm calling 911," Cassandra repeated. It was a good plan and she was sticking to it. She punched in the numbers and waited.

Merlin's brow furrowed; his eyes narrowed; his shoulders hunched; his hands balled into fists. His voice was like the roaring of a hurricane, "I need a door!"

Merlin blinked and stared up at the largest castle drawbridge he'd ever seen. Cassandra gaped, not hearing the emergency operator come on the line. Shocked, William stopped crying and stared at the tremendous wooden bridge.

Merlin stepped up to the drawbridge then paused. On second thought, he didn't like the idea of barging in the front door. "No," he whispered. "Not a door. Something small. So she won't see me coming —"

With no sound at all and in less time than it took Cassandra to say, "Hello," into the phone, the drawbridge disappeared.

A glinting of sunlight caught Merlin's eye and he looked up to see a small open window. Michael's bedroom window. Merlin looked and saw the path. Like magic footprints, he saw the route: the fence, the trellis, the tree, the window. Without a word, or a look back at Cassandra, he began to climb.

Cassandra and William watched Merlin scale what had become a solid fortress up to its one weakness. "Please send help. Thirty-three Cedar Drive," Cassandra said into the phone. She hugged William tighter, consoling them both.

"Please state the nature of your emergency," the operator's voice sounded small and far away.

Cassandra was considering how to answer the question when William answered it for her, "Fire! Mommy said fire. Mommy went to get Michael. Mommy! I want my Mommy!"

"Fire," Cassandra said into the phone, coming out of her reverie. "There are two —" Cassandra looked up and saw Merlin slip quietly in through the open window, "— three people trapped inside. Please hurry."

Cassandra hugged and rocked William who was now crying louder than ever. She looked up and saw the one small window disappear, leaving no trace of its existence in the cold stone face of the impenetrable wall.

Merlin stood in the centre of Michael's room. Smoke twisted upward from the outlets and rose like a dark mist from the flat surface of the walls. The light bulbs in the lamps had shattered, exposing their still crackling sockets. A dark cloud hung above the room, biting Merlin's throat when he breathed. From the hall came the numbing cry of smoke detectors.

Merlin bent down low and made his way toward the sound. He hadn't thought to look at the floor; he hadn't noticed that the carpet was laced with flowing strands of liquid electricity. He didn't get more than two steps before his foot touched one.

A magical electric tongue licked Merlin's foot then instantly clamped itself around his ankle — like the snapping shut of a great bear trap. The magic recognised him and released the natural violence of the electricity it had consumed. Merlin fell to the floor with the jolt.

Electric pulses, like a coded message, surged along the tendril. Their call reverberated through the magic like a drum: "He is here! The one we seek! Come! Come!"

Throughout the house the rivers and streams and pools of electricity undulated with the rhythm of the call and began to flow toward their intended prey. Some flowed up the stairs; others dripped from the attic; still others changed their course and flowed like an impending tidal wave along the upstairs hall.

Morgan Le Fay's pulse raced, urging the magical electricity onward. She was euphoric: Merlin had stepped into the snare, and the boy was slowly suffocating. She would get them both!

18

Mrs. Halsey managed to catch her breath. The pain in her wrists and knees was lessening. She realized the electricity was flowing away from her.

She looked around and saw that the tendrils of sizzling liquid were moving toward the stairs. With sudden panic she looked to Michael. He lay motionless on the bottom step: an easy target. But the coursing fingers of energy passed right by him, bending in sudden angry zigs and zags to go around him, as if annoyed he was in their way.

Upstairs, Merlin was on his hands and knees, panting. Thousands of little shocks ran through him as the electric tongues spiraled their way up his arms and legs. He waited for the imminent explosion in his brain, but it didn't come.

Something was wrong. Morgan could sense it through the protective whirlwind that surrounded her. She felt the angry magical energy growing tired — it was weak from its battle with the electricity. Too weak to defeat its intended foe.

Merlin rallied his strength and got to his feet. The electricity leaked away into the air around him, seizing its chance to escape.

Merlin lurched to the banister and looked down the stairs into a rolling cloud of smoke and noise. He heard Mrs. Halsey calling — her voice choked with smoke and pain and fear, "Michael!"

Air. They all needed air. No. Not just air. Wind. Merlin closed his eyes and concentrated. Then he felt it: the barest caress of a breeze. Somewhere at the bottom of the stairs was enough wind to blow all this smoke up and out the chimney.

Morgan Le Fay felt the first thin thread of wind unravel itself from her spinning shield of protection. She looked toward the upstairs landing. Though she could not see him, she knew Merlin was up there, pulling the wind toward him. Morgan watched as the wisp of air parted the smoke in answer to his call. She watched it clean the air around the woman and her son. She watched it brush Merlin's cheek in a cool, refreshing kiss.

Morgan screamed, and the sound drowned every other sound in the house. Her fury consumed her — fury mingled with fear: the boy still clung to life, and her magical attack had spent its power before its time — leaving Merlin untouched. And now her protection was spinning away into a vortex at Merlin's command.

Merlin looked down through the growing hole in the swirling, thinning smoke. He saw Mrs. Halsey reach Michael and cradle her unconscious son in her arms. She moved as though the effort caused her great agony; she clutched Michael to her with her arms — her hands hanging useless at her wrists.

Merlin looked over and saw the source of the wind, the source of Michael's danger, the source of Mrs. Halsey's pain. He watched as Morgan Le Fay spun like a crimson top at the centre of a tornado.

Merlin realized that once the force of the wind was released, she would be free. There wasn't much time. The smoke was already billowing upward and out through the chimney. The air was becoming breathable, and the smoke alarms were shutting off.

Merlin raced down the stairs to help Mrs. Halsey. She struggled to her feet, her boy limp in her arms. Merlin reached them and tried to take Michael from his mother's waning grasp. She jerked Michael away, fiercely clasping her boy to her chest. Merlin acquiesced, putting his arms around them both, steadying and supporting the two as one.

Merlin knew that Mrs. Halsey was exhausted. He looked upstairs. The climb was too far. He looked around, but there was no other way out. He looked back at Morgan — they were out of time.

Morgan Le Fay's hair and dress settled down around her as smooth and straight as if they'd never been ruffled. She looked at Merlin and waited.

Nothing happened. He must be using all of his energy to help the boy and the woman. His compassion would be his undoing. She had just enough strength left to muster one last attack. It would be ugly, but it would get the job done.

Merlin closed his eyes and imagined the great castle draw-bridge he'd seen before. Beside him, Mrs. Halsey gasped, and he knew the door had materialized. He gave the large metal pulley a nudge with his mind and the great wheel began to turn, releasing the heavy rope and lowering the massive wooden bridge.

Morgan touched her necklace.

Merlin saw a smile cross Morgan's face. He grabbed Mrs. Halsey by the arm and ran toward the lowered drawbridge. A scream erupted above their heads as the sharp spikes of a massive portcullis sliced down towards them from the top of the stone archway. The deadly mechanism speared the floor only centimetres from their toes.

Merlin and Mrs. Halsey stood frozen. Mrs. Halsey was trembling. The sleeve of Michael's shirt had been sheered away by one of the spikes.

Merlin spun around to face Morgan, but she was gone.

Mrs. Halsey moaned. Her head was spinning.

Merlin waved his hand and the heavy black spikes became a colourful bead curtain.

Mrs. Halsey felt Merlin urging her forward. She looked up at his face. For the first time, she noticed what a good face it was. There was something kind in the pale grey eyes, something wise in the high, furrowed brow, and something strong in the set of his jaw. Funny, she'd always thought he had a rather plain, uneventful face. She sank against him and let him guide her through the beads, across the drawbridge and into her own backyard.

19

In the backyard, Cassandra and William saw the heavy wooden drawbridge drop with a thud to the grass. They watched as the portcullis fell and the beads were swept aside. Merlin and Mrs. Halsey, with Michael in her arms, stumbled out into the fresh air of the bright day.

Before Mrs. Halsey could focus her eyes enough to see the pure joy on William's face, she was startled by a loud cry — like the screech of an angry bird. Merlin, Cassandra and William looked up to the top of the house, to the source of the cry.

They turned just in time to see Morgan transform herself into a pitch-black raven. She lifted off the roof and wheeled toward the south. Her guttural "caw" hung in the air, merging with the growing whine of approaching sirens.

William struggled out of Cassandra's grip and ran to his mother. He threw his arms around her legs and hugged her with all his strength. Mrs. Halsey sank painfully to her knees and nuzzled into her baby's love, clutching Michael between them. Merlin and Cassandra looked at the house — it had returned to normal.

Mrs. Halsey felt a hand on her shoulder and didn't want to answer it. She didn't want to be called back to the reality of what had just happened — not that she believed any of it was real. In her fear to get her children out of the fire, and with the dizzying effects of the smoke, she must have imagined all sorts of amazing and terrible things.

The hand on her shoulder squeezed tighter. She reluctantly looked up into Merlin's sober eyes and knew that everything she had seen was real.

"She'll be back," Merlin whispered. "She wants the boy. Next time she'll get him."

Mrs. Halsey looked down at Michael, so still and quiet in her arms, and knew the danger had not passed. "Why?" she asked. "Who is she?"

"Her name is Morgan Le Fay." Merlin paused, "I think she wants revenge."

Mrs. Halsey didn't understand, "But Michael's never done anything to her."

Merlin looked down at the unconscious boy. "No, but he reminds her of someone she hates."

"Who?"

The sudden sound of approaching footsteps interrupted Merlin and Mrs., Halsey. They looked up to see firemen rounding the corner of the house. Behind them came two ambulance attendants carrying a stretcher. Painfully, Mrs. Halsey got to her feet, Michael still draped across her arms.

The ambulance attendants set the stretcher down. The first attendant tried to pull William away from Mrs. Halsey. The second held out his arms to take Michael.

With a rush of foreboding, Mrs. Halsey turned to Merlin. She looked into his eyes and knew he had spoken the truth. She turned back to the ambulance attendant and saw, in her mind: Michael in a safe hospital room hooked-up to a life-giving I.V. Then the vision changed; she saw Michael trapped in that room, tied to an I.V. like a sitting duck.

In less than a heartbeat, she turned and held Michael out to Merlin. "Take him," she said between tears.

Merlin gently scooped Michael up into his arms. He was just turning away when he was bumped from behind. Mrs. Halsey had tried to grab his sleeve, but she couldn't make her hand move; instead, she had bumped him with her forearm. "Bring him back," she added in a hoarse whisper, her throat aching from trying to hold back the sobs.

Merlin nodded gravely, fully understanding and accepting the responsibility. Mrs. Halsey closed her eyes and collapsed into the waiting arms of the second ambulance attendant.

Cassandra had overheard the entire exchange and now watched as Merlin carried Michael around to the far side of the house, toward his waiting car. The ambulance attendants were too busy with Mrs. Halsey and William to notice that Merlin wasn't carrying the boy to their waiting ambulance.

Cassandra caught up with Merlin at the curb. He looked at her — ready to defend himself, but she said nothing. She simply opened the car door and helped to make Michael comfortable in the back seat. Merlin saw that she had chosen not to intervene. He smiled, grateful.

"Where will you take him?" she asked.

He looked northward to the mountains.

Cassandra understood. Merlin had spent much of his youth exploring the wilderness areas of Vancouver Island. Somewhere in a familiar forest, Merlin would find a safe hiding place.

She nodded farewell and whispered, "Good luck."

20

Dr. Cassandra Westinghouse sat in Victoria General Hospital's emergency room, waiting for news about Mrs. Halsey and her son.

Mr. Halsey had been notified and was now in with his wife, holding her hand, desperately trying to understand what she was trying to tell him. So far, her story made no sense: liquid fire, a woman in a red dress, and something about a giant drawbridge. Again, he asked her about Michael. Again, she said only, "He's safe."

John Merlin took the Trans-Canada Highway north, careful not to exceed the speed limit. All of the windows were rolled down, and the warm, refreshing air rushed over his face. By the time he reached Nanaimo, he had a plan fully worked out in his mind. They would continue along the coast on highway 19 past Courtenay and on up to Campbell River where they would take highway 28 west toward Strathcona Provincial Park. Merlin had hiked the park extensively with his adopted father when he was a boy, and then again as a teenager in the park's "Wyld Adventures" summer wilderness program.

Merlin had always felt safe in the park amid the towering Douglas Fir trees. The ancient giants always seemed to welcome him with feelings of gentleness and friendliness. Although Merlin longed to hide in the park, his goal lay just outside of Strathcona's northern boundary. As a boy, he'd spent many hours pouring over park maps, and one spot had always intrigued him: a circle with a dot inside indicating a fire lookout tower. Whenever Merlin had felt scared or lonely, he'd make secret plans to runaway to the tower. He had never actually tried it, though. He did ask a park guide about it once, but the guide had said that particular tower had been abandoned long ago.

Merlin thought of the abandoned tower now as a remote, defensible place where they could hide, watch, wait, and plan . . . if they could reach it in time.

Merlin looked over his shoulder: Michael lay sleeping in the back seat, rocking gently to the rumble and motion of the car. The boy hadn't woken since collapsing on the stairs in his house amid the smoke and noise and mayhem. As Merlin drove, he planted a dream into Michael's sleep. A dream of cool breezes and clear mountain streams, of cleansing things and healing things. As Michael dreamed, his breathing became deeper, more regular. Merlin pictured a clean set of lungs, healthy bronchia, and a mind and body free of the damaging effects of smoke inhalation.

A large black raven collapsed on the rooftop of a downtown shopping centre. The dark shape of the bird shimmered as it slowly changed into a woman — her long black hair fanned out like wings over a blood-red dress. Morgan Le Fay had barely enough strength left to crawl into the shadow of an air conditioning vent. She sprawled on the tar and pebble surface, panting.

She looked up into the clear night sky and saw the stars. They looked just like little candle flames. Merlin's words came back to her, "A string of candles lighting the way to the future." She closed her eyes to shut out the sight. Dizzy and exhausted, Morgan let go of consciousness and slipped into a deep black well of dreamless sleep.

In the town of Campbell River, Merlin turned west onto highway 28, but instead of following the eastern shore of Upper Campbell Lake, he turned onto an old logging road. From there, he knew he could take a series of narrow dirt roads up to Myra Lake. From Myra Lake it would be a short hike out of Strathcona Provincial Park and into the National Forest where they could look for the fire tower. Lacking a map, he'd have to follow the rivers and his memory.

Up ahead, on his right, a sideroad turned north. Merlin got ready to take it, but as he drove closer, he saw that a barricade had been erected across it. A large yellow sign displayed a "natural hazard" warning. Merlin stopped the car and stared at the sign. This was not good. He thought about following the logging roads on foot but the terrain was mountainous. He looked over his shoulder at Michael sleeping in the back seat — the boy was in no shape for hard climbing. He decided to take the longer, but easier, route through Tlools Valley. Merlin looked eastward, if they followed this road to the point where Elk River met up with Tlools Creek, they could hike northward along the lush valley floor to Myra Lake.

Merlin followed the logging road into the park and stopped where the river met the creek. He parked the car on the shoulder and turned off the engine. From here on in, they would have to travel on foot.

Merlin stuffed everything useful he could salvage from his trunk into an old duffel bag. With the bag slung over one shoulder, he gently lifted Michael out of the car and carried him into the woods. He walked slowly, his burden heavy. They wouldn't get far tonight.

21

John Merlin found a sheltered hiding place beneath several closely growing grand fir trees. The little area was surrounded on all sides by the lush foliage of sword ferns. On top, it was roofed by the arching branches of an old western hemlock. It was the kind of place that children chose for secret forts. Merlin would have passed right by had it not been for the rustling of a grouse.

He lay Michael on a soft bed of fallen leaves. The boy roused for a moment, called for his mother, then fell back into a healing sleep. Merlin sat down heavily beside him. He pulled two ragged car blankets from the duffel bag, covered Michael with one, and wrapped the other around his tired shoulders.

An empty bottle of Evian spring water, a flashlight, a brand new box of wooden matches, and a large tin of ancient shortbread cookies (a Christmas gift from Mrs. Fitz-Gardner): Merlin shook his head as he peered into the duffel. It wasn't much. The shortbread would last them for a while, and he could use the tin container for boiling water and cooking. Merlin sighed. How was he supposed to keep Morgan Le Fay at bay with these meager items?

No. Fighting Morgan was not his plan. He wouldn't risk it; he wouldn't risk Michael's life. The fire tower was a four day hike from here. His real enemy was time. Merlin closed his eyes. He was exhausted, desperate for sleep, but his mind wouldn't let him rest. The events of the past two days spun in his head. Had he done the right thing bringing Michael here? Was he really Merlin the Magician? Or was he merely John Merlin the fool?

Maybe Ms. Sanchez had simply fallen and hit her head. Perhaps his knitting had produced nothing more than a hat. Probably the beautiful visitor to his class was exactly who she had said she was and nothing more. After all, electrical fires happened all the time, and the lack of oxygen in all that smoke could have made him imagine anything.

Merlin thought about Ms. Sanchez. He was certain that he was responsible for her recovery. But how? He'd never been able to do anything like that before. Why now? Merlin grew cold. He looked up into the dark canopy. The branches were so thick he couldn't see the stars. All was darkness.

22

Mrs. Halsey was awake and feeling much better. Mr. Halsey sat at the foot of her bed telling her bits of good news: William could go home today; the insurance company had booked them into a motel and would arrange to rent them a furnished apartment next week; the women's group at their church had dropped off a supply of clothes and blankets. He paused. Mrs. Halsey waited for him to ask her about Michael. She knew he'd spent the night phoning friends and neighbors and had turned up nothing.

In the clear bright light of morning, it was hard for Mrs. Halsey to believe that yesterday had really happened — that she'd given her son into the care of a teacher she hardly knew for a reason that sounded crazy. Just then, a small breeze blew the door to her room open just wide enough for her to catch a glimpse of a nurse with long black hair standing in the corridor.

Mrs. Halsey froze, terrified. She looked at her husband, "She's here! The woman in the red dress! She's after Michael! Just like I told you!"

Mr. Halsey was at his wife's side in an instant, stroking her shoulders, trying to calm her, "Cecelia, darling, please. It's all over."

"She started the fire. I know it."

"Started the fire! Why would anyone want to do that?"

Mrs. Halsey wanted to scream that the woman was trying to kill Michael, but that didn't make any sense, and she knew it. She let her voice trail off to nothing.

The expression in her husband's eyes was unmistakable. "There's someone I'd like you to talk to, sweetheart. I met her in the lobby. Maybe she can help you."

Mrs. Halsey sank into her husband's arms. It was no use. Her memory of the fire was all mixed-up. She was certain about the woman being there — and she was certain Mr. Merlin had saved them. But did a gigantic drawbridge really appear? In her desperation to protect her children, she might have imagined anything.

Mr. Halsey gave his wife a hug and a kiss then went to the door. Mrs. Halsey watched him closely; she stiffened as he opened the door.

Mrs. Halsey held her breath, half-expecting a red and black rush of violence. Nothing happened. The hallway was empty. Mr. Halsey leaned out and beckoned to someone.

In the hall, Dr. Cassandra Westinghouse stood staring at the elevator. The doors were just closing on a remarkably beautiful nurse with long black hair. It was neither the nurse's beauty nor her hair that had caught Cassandra's attention: it was the charm around her neck.

Inside the elevator, Morgan marvelled at the device — a metal box for raising and lowering people. Morgan understood the use of levers, wheels, pulleys, wedges, and inclined planes, both straight and circular. A drawbridge used a lever and a pulley to raise and lower heavy wooden planks; pulleys could be used to propel people forward as with Michael's chariot; gears could be used to turn a grindstone. Morgan imagined a team of oxen; she thought of a massive counter-weight — whatever it was, something was making this heavy box move. While she was thinking, another passenger in the elevator pressed the letter "G". Morgan saw the little disc light up a bright orange. She smiled. Magic.

The device began to rumble and vibrate. Morgan felt herself descending. Magic and ingenuity working together — Merlin's birthplace was truly a land of wonders. She understood now why he had always kept it secret.

23

Michael sat bolt upright and called out, "Mom!" He blinked his eyes into focus and stared at his strange surroundings. His mouth was dry, and his throat hurt. The last thing he remembered was his mother calling for him to keep low, beneath the smoke. It must have been a nightmare.

Michael turned all the way around and saw that he was in some kind of leafy shelter. He didn't know where he was or how he'd gotten here. Maybe he was still dreaming. The sound of approaching footsteps interrupted his thoughts. Michael scrambled to the far side of the small shelter. He looked down and saw a heavy stick.

Careful not to spill the contents of the Evian bottle he carried, Merlin pushed aside several bushy branches and ducked into the "fort".

"Oh, good, you're awake," Merlin said as he noticed Michael huddled against the farthest tree trunk, holding the stick out in front of him like a weapon.

Michael stared. The last person he'd expected to see was his science teacher.

"Thirsty?" Merlin asked as he held out the water bottle. "It's still warm; I decided to boil it — some of the water in the park's good for drinking; some's not — giardia lamblia protozoa. Did you know a litre of water can contain as many as fifty million protozoans?" Merlin smiled at the look on Michael's face. He took a drink of water to show that it was safe then once again held the bottle out to Michael. "There's the prettiest little stream not a hundred metres from here."

"Where am I?" Michael asked, taking the bottle. He held it up to the light, imagining he could see the countless microscopic corpses. "Where's my mom? I dreamed our house was on fire. How come you're here?"

Merlin sat down across from Michael. "Your house did catch on fire — but don't worry; your mom and brother are fine. What do you remember about the fire?"

"Not much," shrugged Michael.

"It's important," prompted Merlin.

"Well, I was hiding upstairs . . . I'd sneaked in through my bedroom window — I know, I know, I shouldn't have cut class, but that psycho lady was so boring —" Michael recognized the expression on Mr. M's face: it was the same one he used when he thought a student was avoiding a question. Michael took a sip of water (it tasted good) then continued his story in what he hoped was a succinct and scientific manner, "My mom caught me. Before I could explain, this lady came up behind her. She looked at me . . ."

"And?"

"And that's all I remember. Except for the smoke and noise and my mom yelling for me to keep down. Oh, and one other thing . . ."

"Yes?"

"The lady. She looked familiar."

Merlin nodded.

"Silky red dress and long black hair — hey! She was at the school! She was the one who came when we were catching frogs; she was there when —" Michael couldn't finish; he had a sick look on his face.

"— When Ms. Sanchez got hurt," Merlin finished for him.

"What's going on, Mr. M.? And why are we out in the middle of nowhere?"

"You're here because your mother gave you to me for safe keeping."

"My mother gave me to you? I don't think so! She won't even let me sleep over at Cory's, and he lives next door."

Merlin smiled for a moment then his expression grew somber, "I'll tell you what I think is going on, but you won't believe me."

"Try me."

"Michael," Merlin began, his voice low, "do you believe in magic?"

24

Dr. Cassandra Westinghouse and Mrs. Halsey sat in the chairs by the hospital room window. Mrs. Halsey felt good to be out of bed. She had been talking for some time now, glad to have a listener who didn't look at her like she was hallucinating. Mrs. Halsey smiled at the thought, "The only person who doesn't think I'm crazy is the shrink."

"I understand how you feel," said Cassandra, "and for what it's worth, I think you did the right thing."

"I hope so," said Mrs. Halsey. She lowered her voice to a whisper and added, "She was here."

"I know. I saw her." Cassandra responded.

Mrs. Halsey stared. It was one thing for Dr. Westinghouse to accept her story, it was quite another for her to corroborate it.

"A beautiful woman with long black hair, dressed in a nurse's uniform, wearing a gold and silver serpent necklace," Cassandra said to prove her point.

"Yes," but how —"

"I was in your backyard long enough to see some very strange things. And earlier that day, I saw a woman fitting that description walking toward your house."

"She was looking for Michael," said Mrs. Halsey, "yesterday . . . and today."

Cassandra simply nodded; she knew it was true.

"Mr. Merlin believes she wants to kill Michael."

Cassandra said nothing — she was starting to believe it too. Cassandra gently took Mrs. Halsey's bandaged hands in hers, "I've known John Merlin for a long time. He's very smart. If anyone can figure out what's going on, he can."

Michael leaned against a small western red cedar and tried to catch his breath. He'd run as far as he could, as fast as he could, in the only direction he could think of: away from Mr. M. Michael looked around and found that he was surrounded by the mixed foliage of a second growth forest. He looked west and saw the Insular Mountains; he turned east and recognized the unending string of Coast Mountains. He was in the middle of nowhere surrounded by trees and mountains. He didn't know how to get home from here.

Michael started to cry, then stopped himself by sheer force of will. He was confused and scared, and he didn't believe a word Mr. M. had told him, but he wasn't going to cry. "Merlin the Magician!" Michael thought. Some of the kids had always said he had a screw loose. Now Michael knew they were right.

Michael took a deep breath and was about to start running again when he felt a hand on his shoulder. He spun around and saw Merlin.

"We have neither the time nor the energy to spare," Merlin admonished simply.

Michael easily pulled away from Mr. M.'s gentle grip, "I'm not going with you."

"You don't believe me."

"Why should I? My house caught on fire. It happens. It doesn't mean there's an evil fairy out to get me."

"No, it doesn't. You'll just have to trust me." Merlin lowered his voice, "You saw what she did to Ms. Sanchez. She'll do worse to you."

"Why are you trying to scare me?"

"Because I'm trying to save you."

Michael looked down at the ground. He thought about the blood running through Ms. Sanchez's hair. It made him feel sick inside. "I want to go home," he whispered.

"If you go home, you'll be killed. Your mother knew that. She made a big sacrifice to save you. Don't blow it."

Michael looked at Mr. M. for a long time, half expecting him to break out laughing and tell him it was all a big joke. But Mr. M. had on his "serious face" and Michael knew, deep down inside, he was telling the truth.

25

Merlin and Michael had walked in silence through the forest for most of the day and were both hungry and tired. Merlin had set a hard pace with nothing to offer for sustenance except water and stale shortbread.

Finally, they found a small clearing where they could make camp for the night.

Michael shook out the blankets while Merlin knelt over a small pile of kindling. Merlin held the unopened box of matches in one hand and looked over his shoulder. Michael wasn't watching. Quietly, he whispered to the wood and wished for fire. Nothing happened. He licked his lips and tried again, "Snap and crackle, warmth and light, catch and hold through the cold, dark night." Nothing: no magic came to his call, no power rushed to do his bidding. How had he managed it before? He couldn't remember. Maybe he had used up all his magic . . . maybe he never had any to begin with. Maybe he had been using Morgan Le Fay's own power against her. That would make sense since he'd never been able to do anything magical before her arrival. Maybe she had to be close-by before his magic would work — maybe she had to attack before it would kick in. Merlin looked at the forest all around him. He knew that the true state of nature was not harmony, but balance. Perhaps, magic was the same.

Merlin heard a rustling behind him and turned to see Michael staring at him — fear and accusation clear in his dark eyes. He'd seen Merlin try to light the fire. He'd seen Merlin fail.

"Don't worry about it," Merlin tried to shrug it off. "It probably only works when there's danger nearby — good thing really, we wouldn't want to waste it."

Merlin took out a match and struck it against the side of the box. He looked at Michael and smiled, "We'll just do it the old-fashioned way."

Michael turned his back on Merlin, walked back to his blanket, and sat down with a solid "thump". His situation seemed wholly unbelievable. He folded his arms on his knees and buried his face in the cross of his elbows.

Far away on a rooftop, a shadow stirred. Morgan Le Fay was restless. She had woken an hour ago and had spent that time extending her senses as far as they would reach. Her search proved fruitless — as had her visit to the hospital.

Morgan made up her mind. She would call the creature.

The beast was dangerous and she wasn't certain she had the power to control it, but she could use it to track Merlin — and that was all that mattered.

She closed her eyes and touched her necklace. The rhyme was ancient and difficult. "Come, now, creature born of light and dark," she began. "Spawn of youth and evil! Flicker-tongued head, devouring jaws, slither and run and hiss. Roar with muscles meant for speed on magic hart-shaped feet. Deep within, the call of hounds. The sounds of hunt and kill. Race to me, search for me, in the land of dreams." Morgan Le Fay's silky voice sang the words to the coming night.

Merlin busied himself with cooking their meager meal. He filled the cookie tin with water and made a thin but nourishing soup from the roots and tubers he'd collected along the way. He poured some of the bittersweet soup into the lid of the cookie tin then passed the rest to Michael. The boy took it without a word, without a look. Merlin watched as Michael drank the soup, clearly glad to have it, not even commenting on its unfamiliar flavour.

Merlin knew that Michael was angry; he also knew that the boy was afraid. He would have to think of something to occupy Michael's time, something to get his mind off the craziness of the situation. Merlin watched as Michael drained the last of the soup, set the tin aside, and rolled himself into his blanket. Well, they could start something tomorrow.

Out of the last dying gleam of sunset, the monster raised its head. Its dull eyes swiveled then fixed.

In her mind, Morgan watched the creature lope toward her on a wispy road of clouds. From somewhere deep within the beast came the sound of baying hounds. Merlin could hide the scent of his magic from her, but he couldn't hide it from the Questing Beast. It hunted in the forest of dreams where all such scents lingered.

Morgan formed a picture in her mind of Merlin and the boy; she held it long enough for the creature to taste it deeply. The sound of hounds eager for the hunt bellowed from its bulging belly, and it was off in hungry pursuit of its prey.

Michael was fast asleep. Merlin busied himself with rinsing the cookie tin and dousing the little fire. He scooped handfuls of dirt onto the smoldering embers and stirred them with a stick. For a long time he sat there drawing patterns on the ground, thinking, worrying.

Finally, he lay down on his blanket and looked up at the stars. They looked like little candles scattered carelessly throughout the night. For the first time, Merlin saw the black between the stars; he imagined it growing, covering them, smothering them in its thickness. He thought about how impossibly far away they were. The light from the sun took eight minutes to reach the earth. How long had it taken the light from these stars? Perhaps the stars themselves had already ceased to exist. Merlin allowed himself a small smile: The starts might be gone, but the memory of their light still shone. Merlin rolled over onto his side. He closed his eyes and hoped he would dream of something nice.

26

The beast began its quest by running in an ever-expanding spiral around the building where Morgan Le Fay watched. It sniffed and licked and tasted the delicate currents of thought, searching for the familiar flavour of dreams. When it crossed the Trans-Canada Highway, it paused. It sensed someone sleeping, dreaming . . . of water . . . of air . . .

The beast followed the thin, elusive scent to a gas station where the taste of the dreamer grew rich and thick on its forked tongue. Yes. The boy had been here. Had dreamed here. The creature looked up toward the hills, and deep within its belly, forty hounds howled.

Morgan stood at the edge of the rooftop and looked toward the highway, toward a distant gas station she could not see, toward the distant mountains no more than shadows against the night. Every fibre of her soul vibrated with the baying of the beast. It had picked up their trail. It would follow them. It would find them.

Morgan quickly ducked inside the building and hurried down the stairs. Out on the street, she simply started walking.

John Merlin tossed and turned in his sleep. The night had become uncomfortably warm. A southerly breeze had come up out of nowhere and was blowing over him in tepid gusts like the breath of some great animal. He kicked at his blanket until he was free of its choking heat. A moan escaped his lips, but he did not wake. Quietly, he slipped back down into the deeper recesses of sleep.

Michael was not so lucky. The comfortingly empty layers of deep sleep eluded him. He seemed tied to the rocking, bucking whims of wildly whipping dream fragments. His mind was full of visions of fire and smoke when a new terror opened its eyes and looked into his dreaming mind. Michael wanted to scream, wanted to run, but his body was flooded with sleep. He couldn't move. He was trapped. A wet thought licked his mind and he dreamed he was being tasted.

Morgan walked along the shoulder of the highway, occasionally illuminated by the headlights of passing cars. Suddenly, her vision blurred and she stumbled. She crouched on the gravel and smiled; the beast had found them. She closed her eyes and saw her prey through the creature's eyes: asleep in the open — helpless.

"Ahhhh!" Michael screamed.

Merlin sat bolt upright. He turned to see Michael thrashing about in his blanket. The boy cried out again, caught in the throes of some terrible nightmare. Merlin hurried to his side, took him by the shoulders and shook him gently, "Michael. Wake up. You're dreaming."

Michael's eyes flew open; he stared at some invisible thing behind Merlin then suddenly twisted to one side — desperate to get away. "No!" he cried.

Merlin looked to the place where Michael had been staring. He saw nothing, but the little hairs on the back of his neck started to rise. There was something there. Something magic. "Michael, wake up. You need to wake up!" Merlin repeated.

All at once, Merlin felt Michael relax. The boy gasped for breath as though he were worn-out from running and wiped his forehead; he was perspiring. He looked up at Merlin, scared and confused, "What . . .?"

"You were dreaming."

"Oh." Michael seemed to accept the explanation without argument though he furtively looked around the campsite just to make sure. All was dark and silent. He looked back up at Merlin, "I dreamed that this . . . thing . . . was hunting us, chasing us. It licked my face . . ." Michael shuddered with the memory.

"What kind of 'thing'?" Merlin asked, stealing a look into the trees.

"I don't know. It was kind of crazy, all mixed up. It had the head of a snake, but its body looked like a cat, no, not a cat, a leopard — but its back-end looked more like a lion . . . and its feet . . . they were really weird, they had hooves like a deer." Michael looked up at Merlin and forced a smile, I guess it's just my mind trying to work out all the strange things that have happened in the last two days. That's what my mom would say . . ." Michael's voice trailed off, and his smile faded. He wished his mom was here instead of Merlin.

Merlin gave Michael a reassuring pat on the back and said, "Your mom would be right — it was just a bad dream; there's nothing to be afraid of."

Morgan Le Fay quickened her pace. She had seen, in her mind, where Merlin and the boy lay sleeping; she doubted they would move until daylight. That left her another three or four hours of travelling time.

She was debating whether or not to spend a little magical energy to hasten her progress when two bright lights roared up behind her. She turned and saw dust and gravel being churned into the air as a big rig rumbled onto the shoulder.

Morgan backed toward the bushes beside the road. She knew the thing barreling down on her was some kind of wagon for hauling goods and not a monster, but she raised her hand to her necklace just in case.

The big rig came to a grinding halt amid a cloud of dirt and stones. The passenger-side door swung open and a well-muscled, well-tanned man in his late thirties leaned out, "Awfully late for you to be out walkin'. How's about a lift?"

Morgan smiled and gracefully climbed up into the cab.

The warm wind was gone, and the night had turned cold. Merlin searched the impenetrable shadows all around them but could see nothing. Michael had described a mythological monster called the Questing Beast. In its stomach were said to be forty hunting dogs, all eager to run down their prey. Merlin cocked his head and listened for the sound of baying hounds.

The forest was silent. Merlin didn't tell Michael that he recognized the creature of his dream, that it had a name, that it had probably been sent by Morgan Le Fay. He looked at his watch; it was three a.m. Merlin noticed that Michael was also looking at his watch. "It's very late, you should go back to sleep. I'll keep watch."

"I can't go back to sleep," protested Michael. "Not now!"

Merlin knew that Michael was right. He also knew that they couldn't strike camp until daylight. Maneuvering through the woods at night was asking for trouble. Besides, they both needed the rest. Michael was more exhausted now than he'd been at dinner time. But how could they avoid a creature that hunted in dreams?

Merlin needed to direct their dreaming — away from the beast, along paths it could not track.

"Maybe you could tell me a story," Michael suggested.

Merlin smiled, "I have a better idea. How about a lullaby?"

Michael grimaced. Merlin continued undaunted. He pulled his blanket around his shoulders and looked up at the stars, "Have you ever heard Wagner's four part opera, 'The Ring of the Nibelung'?"

Michael groaned, "The ring of the what?"

"Nibelung. Oh, it's beautiful . . . riveting . . . it takes your mind on an exotic journey to Nebelheim — a magical place where a great treasure is guarded by a brave hero. It tells the story of how the treasure was stolen." The piece, Merlin knew, was hypnotic. It was also very long and would easily carry them to sunrise.

As Merlin continued his description of the opera, Michael looked up at the stars and yawned. His eyelids grew heavy. He imagined that he could actually hear the music Merlin was describing. The rich sounds of the string section: violins, violas, cellos, and double basses, filled the night. Michael curled into a ball beneath his blanket and let the soothing waves of music carry him away.

Merlin paused in his narration, he too could hear the music. The swirling melody rose and fell in delicate adagios and rousing cadenzas. Merlin looked around. The music was real; it filled the forest with sound -- somewhere, something was making the air vibrate. Magic? It was almost as if an invisible orchestra was floating overhead, performing for a tiny audience of two.

Merlin looked over at Michael and saw that the boy was already fast asleep. Confident that their dreams would ride the rhythms of the music, Merlin lay back on the soft leaves and worried. It was important that he find a way to put some normalcy back into Michael's life. But how? Merlin closed his tired eyes, their lids thick and heavy with the emotional effects of the music. He let the sound waves crash against him, wash over him, and carry him toward sleep.

Merlin felt a chill creeping into his hands and feet and cuddled deeper into his blanket; he wished he'd relit the little fire. Behind him, the little pile of long dead embers burst into life — pushing back the darkness and spreading a comforting warmth over the two sleepers.

The Questing Beast ran in circles. It stopped again and again to taste the delicate vibrations of a dreaming world. Now and then, for the briefest instant, it would catch a whiff of the dream current it sought, but as quick as the tingling sensation came, it was gone. Not just gone, but swept far away by some indefinable maelstrom. The beast's confusion deepened and its belly howled in frustration. It had lost the scent of its prey.

27

Merlin woke with a start. The sun was already well up in the sky. They'd overslept.

Merlin quickly rolled up his blanket and packed it into the duffel bag along with their other items. He grabbed the end of Michael's blanket and pulled it off the sleeping child with a "snap".

"Hey!" Michael shouted as he grabbed for the blanket. He sat up and rubbed his eyes.

Merlin shook Michael's blanket, rolled it, and stuffed it into the duffel. "Better get a move on, you don't want to be late," Merlin said as he shouldered the duffel bag.

"Late? What's going on?"

Merlin started into the forest, calling over his shoulder, "School! It's Friday — that's a school day." He stopped and looked back at Michael, "You didn't think I was going to let your education suffer just because we're in the middle of nowhere running away from an evil sorceress who's trying to kill us, did you?"

Michael grimaced: just when he thought things couldn't get any worse.

Merlin smiled, "Come on, the stream's this way. You'd be surprised how good shortbread tastes in the morning."

Michael followed his "mad" science teacher to the stream, splashed some cold water on his face and ate some of the stale shortbread. Mr. M. was right, it did taste better in the morning.

Merlin stood on the bank of the fast-flowing stream and scanned the woods around them. Michael watched and stiffened. Mr. M. was tense; Michael could see it in his shoulders, his eyes. Michael stuffed the rest of the shortbread into his mouth, wiped his hands on his jeans, and hurried over to stand beside his teacher.

Merlin and Michael both gazed into the swiftly moving water. Merlin cleared his throat and in his best "lecture" voice asked, "If you were an animal being hunted, and you didn't want to leave any tracks, but you couldn't fly, what would you do?"

Michael looked down at his brand-new Nikes — his toes curled up in anticipation of the cold water, "I'd walk where my tracks wouldn't show."

"Good, so would I," Merlin said and promptly stepped into the shallow stream. The small stones were slippery under his feet. It would be slow going, but they could make up the time later. "Come on."

Michael shrugged and jumped in with both feet, splashing Merlin to the knees. Merlin's eyebrows raised to his hair line.

"I didn't figure I had a choice," Michael explained.

Merlin laughed out loud. He turned and started to make his way up stream. Michael followed, slipping a little now and then but quickly learning how to place his feet on the unstable pebbles.

As they walked, Merlin talked about the plants around them, the trees above them, and the soil beneath them. Michael listened — partly to Mr. M., partly to the splashing sound his Nikes made. Mr. M. was saying something about soil being like human skin, endlessly forming — being destroyed and renewed. Michael wasn't sure, but he thought he heard Mr. M. say soil came from rocks, that lichens made tiny cracks in the rocks with acid that allowed moss to move in.

Other plants lived and died in the moss, helping it to spread. It all sounded pretty yucky and took a really long time. Then Mr. M. said something that sounded like "liverwort" which reminded Michael of "liverwurst" which reminded him that he was still hungry. Shortbread cookies gave you quick energy, but they sure didn't fill you up.

The tree cover was dense near the stream; Michael noticed that Merlin was picking berries from the close-growing bushes as he walked. Michael started to do the same, careful to pick only those that Mr. M. picked and to ignore the others.

Merlin noted Michael's mimicry with satisfaction and continued his lesson, "What can you tell me about the leaves on these bushes?"

"Uh, they're green —" Michael answered without thinking, instantly wincing at the simplicity of his answer.

Merlin smiled, "Why green?"

Ha! Michael knew this one: "Chlorophyll — they use it to make food."

"From what?"

"From sunlight."

"Ah," said Merlin, "the first link in the chain. What else do you see?"

This time Michael looked closer at the leaves of the bushes, "They're kinda big."

"And the leaves on the trees?"

Michael looked up, "Smaller."

"Why?"

"Why?" Michael repeated.

"I asked you first," Merlin chided.

Michael looked up at the trees and thought about the question.

Merlin splashed onward, quietly picking berries and a few herbs. He had all day to wait for Michael's answer. As long as the boy was thinking about leaves, he wasn't worrying about Morgan Le Fay. Merlin, on the other hand, had been thinking about her ever since he'd mentioned the food chain. He had the disturbing thought that he and Michael might no longer be at the top.

28

A big rig pulled onto the narrow shoulder of Highway 28, on the western shore of Buttle Lake, just in front of the Strathcona Provincial Park Headquarters. The passenger door opened, and a beautiful woman with long black hair hopped out. She smoothed her red dress and looked around. Up ahead, Morgan saw a log cabin with a sign, "Park Headquarters". She strolled toward it, not giving the truck or its driver another thought.

Inside the station, a young park manager, Marty Silverhorn, sat drinking his morning coffee. The door opened and a beautiful woman walked into the station and up to the counter. Marty spilled his coffee in his rush to stand up. She wasn't dressed for camping or even for a day hike. She looked more like she was ready for a night on the town. Marty hadn't seen Morgan get out of the truck, he'd been struggling with a package of coffee stir sticks at the time, so he assumed she must have had car trouble and needed help. "Good morning," he sang as he wiped coffee from his shirt.

"Good morning. I need your assistance."

"You've come to the right man. I can fix a flat, or I can call for a tow. What's the trouble?"

Morgan didn't understand what the young manager had said, so she ignored it and started her story, "My brother and his son are here — in the park —"

"Father and son camping trip," Marty interrupted, "we get a lot of those. It's a good way to spend some quality time with your kid."

"Camping . . ." Morgan pronounced the unfamiliar word with her haunting accent. A tingle rose up Marty's spine. "Yes, they are camping, but they forgot the boy's medicine. Can you provide me with directions?"

"Sure can." Marty walked over to the large wall-map of the park and put his forefinger on the red "you are here" spot. "Which campground were they headed for?"

"I don't know the name, but I know the place . . ." Morgan described Merlin's campsite as she had seen it through the Questing Beast's eyes. She stared into Marty's eyes as she spoke, planting a picture in his mind.

Marty stared back, his eyes blank. He could see the campsite. He recognized it: the lay of the land, the sway of the trees, the path of the nearby stream. He'd been there before. Strange, the woman's mouth didn't seem to be moving — though he heard her liquid voice clearly in his mind. His finger began to trace a path along the map. Morgan watched Marty's finger stop at a spot just below the words "Tlools Lake".

Satisfied, Morgan Le Fay left the cabin without another word. She headed into the forest. It would take her hours to reach the campsite — even then, she would still be a full day and a half's travelling time behind Merlin. Morgan knew many ways to traverse a forest quickly, but they would have to wait. The trick of entering the ranger's mind had weakened her.

29

Merlin decided it was time to leave the stream. He stepped out onto dry land and called back to Michael, "Come on, let's see if we can put in a few more kilometres before lunch."

"A few more kilometres?" Michael thought; he was really hungry now, and his stomach was starting to growl.

Michael climbed out of the stream and followed his teacher; his feet felt icky in his waterlogged socks and shoes, but if Mr. M. could take it, so could he. He'd figured out the answer to Mr. M.'s question about the leaves a while back: the leaves on the bushes were bigger because they lived in the shade of the trees above them — so they had to do something to catch more sunlight. The trees, on the other hand, were in the direct line of fire from the sun, so they had to be careful not too lose too much moisture while catching their rays. Michael thought of the towering Douglas Firs and their great spreading boughs of green needles — but really a needle was just a type of very narrow leaf. Mr. M. had seemed to approve of Michael's answer, but then, suddenly and without warning, he'd turned on Michael with the "big" word, the "scary" word, the word no one in any of Mr. M.'s classes ever wanted to hear: "Therefore . . .?"

Michael had surprised himself by shrugging and answering simply, "Where you live shapes how you grow." Mr. M. had smiled from ear to ear. And more than that, his whole face had stayed in place. His eyes didn't widen; his eyebrows

didn't rise; he didn't expect anything more. He was satisfied . . . and Michael thought, a little bit proud. Michael was
proud too. He repeated his answer in his mind and found
himself thinking of Trevor.

The playground was abuzz with activity. Everyone was
determined to get their fifteen minutes worth of recess.
Trevor stood in the shadow of the school building watching
P.J. Bazhan go from child to child collecting coins in a big
jar. Several other students were doing the same. When P.J.
passed near to him, Trevor called out, "What'cha doin'?"

P.J. turned to him, "Collecting money for Michael Halsey's
family. Their house burnt down, you know. We're going to
take it to them at the Pacific Motor Lodge after school."

Trevor stared at the jar of money in her hands.

P.J. caught his gaze and hugged the jar to her chest, "Don't
even think about it!"

During their morning "hike" Merlin and Michael had
reached a section of old growth forest. The mild, wet climate
here created a coastal rainforest effect, encouraging massive
growth. Michael stood amid the seemingly endless stand of
Douglas fir trees, marvelling at the towering giants. Merlin,
too, looked up at the tall and mighty trees. He felt their gentle
presence. Here and there, hazy shafts of friendly sunshine
pierced the dark, multi-layered forest canopy with magical
light. Merlin had a particular fondness for the warm yet
unearthly quality of this light.

"Distance, distance," the warning rang in Merlin's mind.
He scanned the forest, searching for the best path to take. He
wished he had the time to hide their footprints — if Morgan

found the place where they had left the stream, she would be on them in no time.

Merlin turned to check on Michael in time to see the smallest of breezes come up — just enough to lightly blow a few dry leaves and some twigs carelessly over two sets of tracks. Michael saw it too. He looked at Merlin and saw the fear in his teacher's eyes. Merlin's magic was working just fine, and that meant only one thing — Morgan was getting closer. They both found the energy to run.

Trevor rode his bike up to the Pacific Motor Lodge. It had taken more than half of "lunch-time" to get here (he'd be in trouble for getting back to school late, but he didn't care). Trevor pulled a large, bulging paper bag out of his newspaper sack, locked his bike, and walked up to room number twelve. The bag was stuffed with something soft, and he tried to smooth out the wrinkles before he knocked.

The door opened, and Mrs. Halsey stepped out. She looked like she'd been crying. She managed a smile and said, "Can I help you?"

"Uh, I'm lookin' for Michael Halsey."

Mrs. Halsey swallowed before she answered, "Michael's not here right now."

"Oh."

"I'm his mother . . ." she added helpfully.

Trevor held out his package, "Could you give him this? It's some clothes. They might be a little big . . ."

Mrs. Halsey smiled and took the gift. "Thank you," she said and meant it.

Trevor nodded. The clothes had been secondhand when his mom had bought them for him, but they were good brands, his mom had an eye for that, and they were clean. Trevor wanted to add that he was sorry about their house and that he hoped they would be okay, but he wasn't good at saying things like that. Instead, he just stood there looking uncomfortable.

Mrs. Halsey stood there too, smiling at Trevor and clutching the paper bag tighter and tighter in her hands. A tear started to roll down her cheek, and Trevor started to fidget. A tall man, Michael's father, appeared in the doorway behind Mrs. Halsey. He gently lead his wife back into the room, closing the door behind them.

Trevor stood there for a moment — something wasn't right. He glanced over at an open window. Quietly, he crept past the door, crouched down and crawled beneath the window sill. Through the screen, he could hear voices inside. Ever so slowly, Trevor inched his head upward until he could see over the sill.

Inside the motel room, Mr. Halsey led his wife to the couch and helped her sit down. He tried to take the paper bag, but she wouldn't release her hold on it.

"Please, honey: they haven't called or anything. I know you believe Michael's safe with Mr. Merlin, but it's been too long. I think it's time we called the police."

Outside the motel room window, Trevor continued to eavesdrop.

"Eh hem!"

Trevor spun around at the sudden sound of a throat being cleared directly behind him.

Dr. Cassandra Westinghouse tapped her foot lightly.

Trevor managed his most innocent-looking smile.

Cassandra smiled back, but she didn't seem pleased. "May I help you?" she asked.

"Uh, no . . ." stuttered Trevor, "I uh, I dropped a quarter."

Dr. Westinghouse didn't say anything. She just stood there, waiting.

"I'll, uh, look for it later . . ." Trevor added.

"Good idea," said Cassandra. She waited for Trevor to move away from the window before she knocked on the door.

Trevor hurried to his bike. He made a big production of struggling with the lock while his eyes remained fixed on suite number twelve. As he watched, the door opened, and the woman disappeared inside.

30

Merlin stopped walking, arched his back, dropped the duffel bag, and turned to look for Michael. The boy was doggedly bringing up the rear: his spirits were dragging and so were his feet. Merlin had pushed them hard. "Let's eat. You hungry?" Merlin called.

"Hungry?" Michael looked up, "I'm so hungry I could eat a bear!"

"Shhh! The bears might hear you," Merlin admonished with a smile.

Michael didn't smile, but he did look around for bears.

Merlin walked over to an enormous tree stump and began dumping out the contents of his pockets. Dozens of berries — mostly blueberries and tiny wild strawberries — spilled out as well as the remaining shortbread cookies. Michael walked over to the tree stump and looked down at the meager offering. He was about to say something but thought better of it. Mr. M. was doing his best. Michael nodded toward the shortbread and berries, "Hey! Two out of four food groups isn't bad! It looks great."

Merlin smiled knowingly, and the two of them sat down to eat. Michael made a blueberry sandwich, using the cookies like slices of bread. The juicy berries made the dry shortbread palatable. "It's good. Try it," Michael said with his mouth full. Merlin followed suit, built his own sandwich, and took a big bite. Merlin nodded his compliments — it was good.

The two of them ate in silence.

Dr. Cassandra Westinghouse sat on the couch beside Mrs. Halsey. Mr. Halsey sat uncomfortably on the chair opposite them. No one looked happy.

"Listen, Doctor. I'm just trying to get this straight. You and Mr. Merlin just happened to be outside our house when the fire broke out?"

"Yes. And your wife gave him permission to take Michael."

"So you said, but don't you find it odd that he hasn't called to let us know where they are, or that they're safe?"

"You don't understand the circumstances —"

"You're right," said Mr. Halsey, glancing sharply at his wife. "I don't. Will someone please explain them to me?"

Cassandra looked at Mrs. Halsey who simply shook her head.

"Dr. Westinghouse," Mr. Halsey said in a very quiet, very calm voice, "was John Merlin your patient?"

Cassandra looked up. She couldn't lie. She looked at Mrs. Halsey, then at Mr. Halsey. She cleared her throat and gave the only answer she could, "That information is confidential."

Mr. Halsey stared at Cassandra. He understood exactly what she had just told him, but he hadn't really been expecting it. He walked over to the couch and sat down beside his wife. He took her hands in his, "Sweetheart, you know I love you — and I'm trying to believe you about the strange woman you saw, but I really do think it's time we called the police. I mean, what if you're right and this woman really is trying to kill Michael? The police would help. Please, I have to know where they are!"

"I know where they are," Cassandra interrupted.

Mr. Halsey and Mrs. Halsey both turned to stare at her.

"I mean, I know where they were headed. I think I could find them."

"I'm coming with you," insisted Mr. Halsey.

"No. Your wife and William need you here. Give me twenty-four hours. If I haven't found them by then, I'll call the police myself."

31

"Is she close?" Michael asked, looking over his shoulder, half expecting Morgan Le Fay to interrupt their meal.

"No. I think we can keep ahead of her . . ." Merlin looked at Michael and saw how tired he was and how scared. Merlin cleared his throat, "Did you know we're sitting in the middle of a time machine? Look around: this is one of the last examples of the kind forest cover that was here before commercial logging began. In Europe, similar forests disappeared centuries ago. Being here is like being in another time." Merlin paused and brushed the cookie crumbs off the tree stump with his hand. "Now, who can tell me how old this tree was when it was cut down?" Merlin looked around the forest as if he were looking around a classroom full of students. "Mr. Halsey?"

"That's easy, all you have to do is count the rings," said Michael, only paying half attention.

"Good. Start counting."

Michael glared at Mr. M. This had all the earmarks of a "make work" project to keep his mind off their troubles. Reluctantly, he put his forefinger in the centre of the stump and started to count.

"From the outside," Merlin corrected.

"What difference does it make?"

"A lot. Out loud, please."

Michael moved his forefinger to the outside edge of the tree stump and began counting rings, out loud. "One, two, three, four, five, six, seven, eight, nine, ten, eleven, twelve —"

"Stop," interrupted Merlin.

"What?" Michael looked up, a little annoyed.

"How old are you?" Merlin asked.

"Twel —" Michael's voice trailed off as he looked down at the tree stump. His finger had barely moved away from the bark.

"This is a Douglas fir. One of the longest living things on earth. Not quite as old as a Sequoia or a Redwood, but old enough."

Michael started counting rings in groups of tens and twenties, estimating his way toward the centre. "There's hundreds of 'em! Maybe even a thousand!"

"Most of the giant trees around us are three to four hundred years old, some are as much as eight hundred." Michael looked at the trees all round him with new respect.

Merlin smiled, "Some of these were already old when Captain James Cook first landed at Nootka Sound in 1778, just a few kilometres from the park's western edge."

Michael was impressed, "Too bad they can't talk," he mused.

"But they can."

Michael turned to Mr. M., his eyes narrowing in a "Yeah, right," expression.

"Look at the rings again. What do you see?"

Michael looked, "They're kind of wobbly."

"What else?"

Michael studied the rings like a puzzle. Finally, he said, "Well, some are close together and others are farther apart."

"Why?"

Michael looked up at Mr. M., exasperated. But before Michael could protest, Merlin expanded his question, "What do the rings represent?"

Michael thought for a moment, "A year in the tree's life."

"More than just time . . ." Merlin coaxed.

Michael's eyes grew wide, he understood, "Size! Each ring shows how much the tree grew in that year."

"Therefore . . .?"

Michael smiled, he was starting to lose his fear of that word. "Therefore," Michael repeated, "some years it grew more than others."

"Now, what would make a tree do that?"

Michael thought about the question. He was excited — being stuck in the woods with a teacher wasn't so bad after all. "Rain maybe, weather, sunshine and stuff. If the tree had lots of water and sun, it would grow a lot. If there was a drought or a real long winter, it might not grow as much." Michael looked up at Mr. M., triumphant. Yes, it was there: the pride in his teacher's eyes.

"Look again," Merlin whispered, "there's more."

Michael looked at the rings, scrutinizing them for hidden meaning.

"Look for a pattern," Merlin urged.

Michael saw it. "Most of the time they're in bunches." He looked at the groups of narrow rings followed by groups of fat ones. "Sometimes only three or four," he continued, "Sometimes as many as eight. This is neat!"

"Now go back to the outside edge," said Merlin, "What's the last thing you see?"

Michael looked at the tree stump, "A group of fat rings. Eight of them . . ."

Merlin looked at them too, "Therefore . . .?"

Michael smiled proudly, "The next one'll probably be narrow."

"Which means?"

Michael's smile faded, he looked up at Merlin, "Hard times are coming."

"See, it's not so difficult to predict the future." Merlin paused then rose slowly to his feet. "Come on, we've rested long enough."

Dr. Cassandra Westinghouse headed for her green Blazer parked in front of the Pacific Motor Lodge. Michael was in no danger from John Merlin — Cassandra would stake her reputation on that. But Michael was in danger, and if anything happened to him, John Merlin would be blamed.

She climbed into her Blazer, gunned the engine and headed for home. Her gear should still be in the basement from her last camping trip. She'd been to Strathcona twice in the last five years and had often talked with John about the park. She had a strong hunch where he was headed.

As Merlin walked, he studied the memory of a map in his mind. If they were where he hoped they were, just south of Myra Lake, there would be a hiking trail just over the next rise. If they followed the trail, they could make better time than walking through the forest. Merlin looked at the sun: it was well past its zenith. Yes. They would take the trail.

32

Merlin and Michael had been following the trail for hours. They had reached the lake and were making their way along its eastern shore. Merlin could see Mt. Evelyn on his right. Tomorrow they would reach the boundary of the park, and with a little luck, would find the fire tower just past Jessie Lake. Merlin was noting the fact that not a single hiker had passed them when he heard Michael zip up his jacket. Merlin felt the chill, too. He looked at his elongated shadow. They had about twenty minutes of light left to find shelter for the night. For some reason, Merlin wanted walls — strong walls all around. He looked up into the sky and could just make out the first few evening stars: their ancient light twinkled as it struggled through the atmosphere.

Morgan Le Fay stood in the centre of the long dead camp-fire and surveyed the site. She ground her delicate heel into the cold ashes and licked her lips. Merlin and the boy had made camp here; their scent still lingered in the air.

She stepped out of the ashes and followed two sets of footprints away from the clearing, over a low rise, down an embankment to a swift but shallow stream. There the trail vanished.

Morgan looked both ways along the streambed: nothing. She looked up at the sky. Night was falling. "Fine," Morgan thought, she could use the rest. Tomorrow, she would use her magic to make up for lost time.

Morgan sat down under a nearby tree and pulled her shawl around her shoulders. She glared at the long-dead campfire — it burst into life with a startled snap. Morgan smiled. Soon she would call the beast.

The call of an owl drew Merlin's attention to the east. He stopped and squinted into the forest. He didn't spot the bird, but he did spot a cabin. It looked old, unoccupied. Merlin turned to Michael and saw that the boy was also looking at the cabin. "Come on, let's see if anybody's home."

Merlin and Michael quietly made their way toward the old logger's cabin. As they drew closer, they saw that it had been abandoned to the elements long ago: the glass was broken out of the one window, pieces of the roof littered the ground, and the door hung precariously from a single rusty hinge. Merlin smiled and turned to Michael, "I believe they have a vacancy."

Merlin soon had the old wood-burning stove going; the cabin felt cozy and safe. Michael curled up on the floor in his blanket while Merlin stood by the broken window looking out at the night. As he watched, the tree branches began to sway with a light breeze. Merlin thought he could just make out a low sound at the very edge of his hearing range. The deep thrumming swish and rustle rose to a higher pitch, as if the wind were blowing stronger, increasing the frequency with which the leaves were vibrating. As Merlin listened, he recognized the clear, distinct tone of a flute. The sweet melody of a lullaby began to form in Merlin's mind.

Morgan Le Fay was out there somewhere, so was the Questing Beast. Merlin pushed the unsettling thoughts away and concentrated on the tune in his head. Brahms. Merlin smiled and imagined an orchestra in the trees. The delicate, lyrical music filled the night. Merlin covered the window with his blanket to keep out the draft; the worn fabric absorbed some of the sound but not enough stop the music's dream-like effect. Merlin stretched out on the floor by the stove.

The Questing Beast sniffed the air and turned in circles. It couldn't catch the scent it wanted. A furious bellow erupted from the creature's innards that echoed up to the very tops of the tall, tall trees.

Morgan Le Fay concentrated on her connection with the Questing Beast. She felt its frustration. It had lost Merlin's and Michael's dream scents. No matter. In the morning, she'd just change herself into something that could track them in the real world — something that could cover the distance between them with speed.

Merlin woke shivering. The fire in the stove had gone out. He sat up and looked for Michael. The boy was not in the cabin. As Merlin started for the door, a sizzling "pop" crackled in the stove — the fire Merlin had fleetingly wished for burst into reality. Merlin stared at the fire then ran for the door, calling, "Michael!"

Outside, Merlin was relieved to see the boy standing nearby, hugging a tree. "Michael . . .?" Merlin asked, curious.

"Yeah?"

"What are you doing?"

"I'm tryin' to figure out what made these marks," Michael explained as he gestured to the scarred tree trunk. "They look like scratches from a big cat. Hey!" Michael spun around to look at Merlin, "Do they have any big cats in the park? Like cougars or mountain lions or . . . or. . . .?"

"Pumas," Merlin supplied the name. He smiled at the boy but not at the scratch marks. "Yes, they have cougars and mountain lions and pumas . . . which, by the way, are just different names for the same kind of cat."

"Oh," said Michael and paused for a moment. "Cougar," he answered. "Cougar's the best."

"Then Cougar it is," Merlin said as he stepped up to the tree, running his fingers along the inside of the scratches. "But these marks weren't made by a cougar; they were made by a black bear."

"How do you know?"

"The scratch marks of cougars are thinner, more shallow. Both bears and cougars claw trees as high up as they can reach to show how big and strong they are. They're just trying to scare away rivals, but the scratches open wounds in the tree for insects and fungus to attack."

"No, I mean how do you know the bear was black?"

Merlin was about to explain that black bears were the only bears indigenous to the island when he saw the wide "gotcha" grin spreading across Michael's face. Merlin realized he was being had and started to laugh. Michael laughed too. It felt good.

33

Morgan Le Fay stretched in the early morning sunlight. Golden fur rippled along her arched back. She shook the morning fatigue out of her muscles, out of her joints, out of her tail. A low rumble grew in her throat. She took a few steps to coordinate her four paws then paused, opened her jaws, and roared.

Morgan felt the tremendous power of the creature she'd become and was satisfied. She padded to the stream and gazed at her reflection. A massive mountain lion stared back at her — magnificent. In this form, Morgan hoped to track, and maybe even catch, Merlin and the boy. If she timed it just right, she could use her frighteningly sharp teeth and claws to kill Michael quickly — leaving her with more than enough energy to tackle Merlin.

The great cat scanned the ground and instantly spotted two sets of footprints leading to the water's edge. She looked downstream — somewhere those footprints would reappear. She bunched the muscles in her powerful hind legs and leapt to the chase, racing along the bank of the stream, devouring the distance between her and her prey.

Merlin and Michael wove their way toward Jessie Lake through a maze of impossibly tall Douglas Firs. The limited, almost ghostly streams of light that filtered thorough the lofty canopy supported little ground cover, making the terrain easy to traverse. Although their morning trek had been effortless, Merlin seemed to grow more nervous, more agitated, with each new step. Suddenly, he started to run.

"What happened?" Michael asked, trying to keep up.

Merlin called over his shoulder, "North of here is an abandoned fire tower — I hope. It's a good place to hide; an easy place to defend." Merlin sped-up even more, "If we can reach it in time."

"In time? Is she that close?"

"Not yet — but she's closing — fast. I can feel it." Merlin headed northward at double time. Michael was right behind him.

Dr. Westinghouse stared at Merlin's old car. She had spent last night in a motel outside of Campbell Lake and had driven the rest of the way this morning. She looked at her watch: 10:00 a.m. If she could find John and Michael's tracks, she might be able to catch up to them before her time ran out. Keeping her attention sharply focused on the ground, Cassandra started searching for footprints.

Merlin and Michael jogged through the forest of gigantic trees. They had found a comfortable pace and were making excellent time. Between deep, rhythmic breaths, Merlin tried to keep his pupil's mind occupied with something other than the fact they were running for their lives. "Scientific name?" Merlin quizzed.

"Pseudotsuga taxifolia . . . Doulasii," Michael exhaled.

"Height?"

"Over sixty . . . metres."

"Circumference?"

"Up to nine . . . metres."

"Diameter?"

"Big! All right? They're big!" Michael yelled.

Merlin smiled but he didn't slow down. The two of them continued on in silence through an isolated stand of western red cedar. Michael was watching the uneven ground, careful not to trip, when Merlin's hand caught him square in the chest.

"What?" Michael asked as he looked up. He breathed a single word, "Oh." They had run out of trees.

Merlin and Michael stared: a few isolated Douglas Firs stood like grave-markers amid a seemingly endless field of stumps.

"What happened?" Michael asked.

Merlin wiped the sweat from his face. "This area must have been harvested, recently."

"Harvested?" asked Michael.

"Logged . . . extensively. Almost every tree's been cut down," Merlin explained as he caught his breath. "Not good — destroys the whole ecosystem — increases all types of erosion."

"What do we do now?"

Merlin looked north: the fire tower was nowhere in sight. He looked behind him at the cedars, at their lightly rustling branches. He looked up at the sun and saw that it was well past noon. He turned and looked south, back toward Myra Lake. The hairs on the back of his neck started to rise. "We're not going to make it," Merlin whispered.

The look in Merlin's eyes sent a shiver up Michael's back. Terrified, Michael took hold of his teacher's shirt-sleeve and tried to pull him toward the tree graveyard. "Come on. Please," Michael urged, "we've got to try."

"No," Merlin said with surprising firmness, "we'll never make it across before nightfall."

"So? When it gets dark, we'll hide."

"Where?" Merlin asked simply.

Michael looked at the scene before him: stumps littered the landscape like discarded bones.

"We'll go back to Myra Lake," Merlin decided with less certainty than Michael would have liked. "We'll hole-up someplace; hide our tracks. She'll pass right by us and keep on going."

"She will?"

"It's better than being caught out in the open."

Michael shook his head; he wouldn't go. He wouldn't take a single step backward, a single step toward the woman who had set his house on fire, a single step toward the woman who wanted to kill him. Michael cleared his throat and tried to sound brave. "Not every tree is gone," he began slowly. Merlin nodded and looked out over the area. The individual Douglas firs were few and far between — here and there stood a lone western red cedar.

"We'll just run from tree to tree," Michael explained.

Merlin managed a small smile. Michael was right. Forward was better than backwards, and he certainly didn't want to face Morgan any sooner than he absolutely had to. Merlin chewed his lower lip as he thought over their limited options. Finally, he said, "I like it," then added in a whisper, "Let's go."

The ground flew by as Morgan Le Fay's powerful paws ate up the shrinking distance between her and Merlin. As she surged through the forest, the thin tendrils of her prey's scent grew thicker, stronger, closer. She leapt across a narrow hiking trail and found her senses flooded with the smell of Merlin's power, the aroma of the boy's life.

Ahead of her stood an abandoned cabin. She slowed her pace and circled it. They had made camp here. Morgan pad-

ded up to the broken door and sniffed. Her great head turned
to the north then up to the sky. It was late afternoon; soon,
night would fall. Morgan allowed herself a deep, resonant
purr — not a problem for a cat.

Merlin and Michael picked their way around the stumps.
They had started out running, but the atmosphere of the place
had slowed them down — it was like walking through the
aftermath of a massacre. Once in a while, they would rest
in the lee of one of the few remaining trees.

Merlin looked at the sky. It was late. Too late. Up ahead
stood the massive shell of a burned-out Douglas fir. He
nodded toward it and called to Michael, "There, we'll make
camp there." He really meant "hide," but "camp" sounded
better — it sounded like they still had a chance.

They reached the blackened hollow tree. Merlin ran his
hand gently over its scarred bark. "Still alive," he whispered
to himself, "alive and standing. Not loggers, not fire . . ."
Merlin crossed his fingers and added silently, "not magic."

Merlin ducked inside the great crack of an opening in
the tree's base. Plenty of room. The floor was soft with dry
leaves and long-abandoned nesting materials. How many
animals had this old tree sheltered? Whatever the number,
tonight it would protect two more.

Merlin leaned out through the opening and beckoned to
Michael, "It's time."

Michael took one last look back the way they'd come.
Nothing moved. He looked at the charred bark of the old
tree and broke off a small piece. It flaked away to nothing
in his hand.

"Hey!" said Merlin, "It's still alive."

Michael looked up, way up, at the few remaining branches,
the scant canopy of leaves. "Barely."

Inside the tree's base, the air was warm and thick with the scents of life and death; sprigs of green poked through the mass of composting forest matter. Merlin made himself comfortable and gestured for Michael to do the same.

Michael sat down slowly. He looked at the black soot marks on his fingers from the crumbled piece of bark. "Fire," he whispered, "it's been in a fire, too."

"They're fairly fire resistant." Merlin paused to pat the interior of the tree, "Their real enemies are Laminated Root Rot and a shallow root system." Merlin saw that Michael had turned to look out at the vast landscape of stumps. "So they have a tendency to topple over."

"What?" asked Michael, his attention back on Merlin.

"Mmm," Merlin nodded, "Sometimes they just fall down."

"Great."

Merlin chuckled, "This tree has stood for hundreds of years. I think it can stand for one more night."

Michael looked at the interior of the tree. It looked strong enough. From somewhere, he thought he could hear music. In front of him, the sun was setting. As he watched, the opening in the base of the tree began to shimmer — shimmer and disappear. Michael looked at Merlin and knew that he was using magic. Using it to heal the tree, to hide them inside, to lull them to sleep, to confuse the beast.

Michael opened his mouth to say something, but Merlin signaled for silence. "If we're quiet," Merlin explained in a whisper, "maybe the tree's life force will hide ours."

Michael stared at Merlin; he'd heard the "maybe" loud and clear. Merlin managed a small smile. Michael managed one in return. Then, as quietly as he could, Michael huddled down into the soft ground and closed his eyes.

Merlin closed his eyes too — for the first time in days, wrapped in the living trunk of the tree, he felt safe.

34

"Come look at this," Michael called.

Merlin poked his head out of the opening in the tree's trunk. He blinked. The sun and Michael were both up. Merlin crawled out of their hiding place and got to his feet. He scanned the woods for danger. He heard Michael talking, but his attention was elsewhere. "Hmmm," was all he said."

"No, look!" Michael grabbed Merlin's arm and turned him to face the tree. "They're so long and so high up — the cougar (Michael stressed the word, showing off that he'd been paying attention) must be gigantic!"

Merlin stared at the fresh, narrow, knife-like scratches. He stepped back.

Merlin heard the panting and froze. He felt the delicate intake and exhale of warm, moist breath. He heard the throaty growl. He turned and saw the yellow eyes trained hungrily on Michael.

The cougar was enormous. Its silky golden fur trembled lightly over softly rippling muscles. It was ready to pounce.

Merlin stole a glance at Michael. The boy stood frozen less than four metres to his right. Four metres: the cat would be on Michael before Merlin could take his first step.

The cat crouched lower, preparing to spring.

Merlin saw the claws — sharp and vicious. He saw the teeth — white and terrible. He saw the animal's hunger; he felt the woman's hate. He saw the amulet — silver and gold wrapped around a blood red stone. He closed his eyes and saw ivory teeth and golden fur wrapped around a blood-red boy.

The cat leaped.

Michael raised his arms to protect himself.

Merlin thought about the only cat he knew. Mrs. Fitz-Gardner's cat. Mrs. Fitz-Gardner's old, fat, lazy orange cat. Marmalade never pounced. Marmalade could barely walk. Merlin heard Michael scream and opened his eyes. He watched the cougar change in mid-flight.

The harmless but heavy house-cat thudded against the boy's upper body. Michael stumbled and fell backwards. The flabby pet landed painfully on all four of its arthritic feet.

Michael opened his eyes, surprised to be alive. Surprised not to have been ripped to shreds. Surprised to see a fat orange house-cat crouching on the ground beside him. But even more surprised to see it smiling.

The marmalade-coloured cat turned its head to look at Merlin. That was all it took. The air cracked like thunder.

Merlin screamed.

Michael turned at the terrifying sound and saw his teacher impaled by a searing bolt of lightning. The bolt entered Merlin's body through his left ear and exited through his right thigh — anchoring him to the earth with a living electric spike. The skin at the entry and exit points sputtered and popped.

Tears streamed from Merlin's eyes. He couldn't move, he couldn't talk, he couldn't think. His muscles had contracted, his heart was racing, and he was having trouble breathing. Magical electricity was slicing through him at 160,000 km per second. Little offshoots from the main bolt followed the paths of his sweat and his tears. He had become a living specimen pinned to a collector's wall.

Morgan purred as she watched the frightening beauty of the magic. She started to hum. She hummed a tune that sounded like falling rain.

Michael looked down at the ground. Water was beginning to percolate up from the earth.

The marmalade-coloured cat was careful not to let its paws touch the water. Michael watched as it sprang up the trunk of the nearby tree. He looked back down at his feet and saw the water reaching for his shoes.

Merlin could smell his flesh burning, but he couldn't do anything to stop it.

He looked at Michael. The boy didn't seem to be in any danger. Merlin looked down and saw the water swirling up out of the earth.

Something about the water was wrong, odd, unnatural. Merlin looked up and saw the orange cat climbing higher into the few remaining branches of the burned-out Douglas fir. He looked back at Michael, at the boy's feet, at the water ready to splash the toes of his brand-new Nikes.

In that instant, Merlin found his voice, "Dry! Dry feet! Dry shoes! Dry land!"

The earth rumbled and shook as an island erupted beneath Merlin and Michael. The water quickly ran down and away from Michael's shoes — down and away from the gently sloping sides of the island. The section of earth rose steadily above the unusually clear, remarkably sparkly water until it reached the approximate size of a baseball diamond.

Up in the tree, Morgan Le Fay licked her lips and shifted her position on the branch. She had shaken off Merlin's annoying bit of magic and returned to human form. She looked at Merlin: his attention was all on the boy, as she knew it would be. By the time he understood the true nature of his danger, it would be too late.

35

High above the spreading water, Morgan Le Fay reached out a slender hand and started tracing an endless circle in the air. The water rose up in response, calling out with bubbles and waves. She ignored it and kept on stirring.

Michael stared at the crackling bolt of lightning still pinning Merlin to the ground. He had to squint against the blinding light to see his teacher. Mr. M.'s face was twisted in pain.

Compelled by an almost morbid fascination, Michael reached out to touch the lightning.

Though Merlin's eyes were closed, he sensed Michael's impending danger. With less breath than it takes to blow out a match, the bolt was gone.

"Ouch!" Michael yelled as Merlin slapped his hand away.

"Don't touch!" Merlin yelled, as if he'd just stopped a toddler from burning himself on a hot stove.

Merlin blinked. It took him a moment to realize that the pain — all of it — was gone. The smell of burning flesh had disappeared with the bolt. He touched his ear, his thigh. His skin was whole. It wasn't even warm. He looked at Michael. The boy was rubbing his hand. The slap had hurt.

Merlin smiled, "Thank you."

"No sweat . . . what happened to the lightning?"

Merlin shrugged, "I couldn't get rid of it, no matter how hard I tried . . . until I thought it was going to hurt you. Then, well, like you said, 'no sweat'."

They were interrupted by a great splashing sound coming from the newly created lake. They turned and saw that the few remaining trees were losing their grip on the land. The soil was being washed out from beneath their roots and they were beginning to topple. One by one, the isolated giants were falling. They crashed into the thirsty water, sank and were gone. All except for the tree on their tiny island. The tree in which Morgan sat.

She swung her legs freely over the edge of the branch. Her laugh was a spiral: spinning, revolving, swirling warm saliva down her throat; spinning, revolving, swirling grass, leaves, branches, whole trees, down the sucking mouth of a great and growing whirlpool.

The little island was in the centre of the maelstrom. The water bit and snapped at its ragged shoreline. As Merlin and Michael watched the earth being eroded away, they heard Morgan start to sing.

Merlin looked up and saw her straddling the branch, arms wide, staring straight at him, "Time and time and time — mine for all time. Time is all mine. You cannot run, but will you age? Forever trapped in your tiny cage."

Morgan's smile was infectious. She was beautiful. "You will play no more tricks with time, Merlin. I still don't know how you brought us here, but here you will stay for time on time on time!"

Morgan's eyes sparkled as she saw the panic wash across Merlin's face. "That's right — I'm not going to kill you. I'm not even going to kill the boy. I'm a fast learner — you told me that once . . . about fifteen hundred years ago."

Morgan's smile faded; she spat into the water. "Fifteen hundred years, Merlin. That's how long you'll be here. I'm not taking any chances. Arthur will not rise because you will not be there to lift him."

Merlin sat down and started to take off his shoes and socks. He said simply, "You're bluffing."

Morgan's eyes flashed.

"There isn't that much magic in the whole world," continued Merlin. "You can imprison me for life, but you cannot extend my life — not by a single minute, let alone fifteen hundred years." Merlin walked to the edge of the island and reached out his foot as if ready to step into the whirlpool.

Morgan caught her breath in anticipation. She stared at his naked foot poised centimetres above the water.

Merlin paused. His eyes narrowed. He pulled back his foot, "Where did you get the water, Morgan?"

Morgan gracefully maneuvered herself into a standing position on the branch. She was majestic as she sprouted wings. A great pair of black wings — raven's wings — flapped gently on her back, testing the breeze. "This little pond?" Morgan crowed as she eagerly answered Merlin's question. "It's Escalonde's bath water."

With that, Morgan flapped her magnificent wings and lifted off the branch.

Michael watched as Morgan pushed with her legs, increasing her thrust against the drag of the air. He stared as the winged-woman defied gravity and flew away. Michael turned to see if Merlin was watching. He saw his teacher gingerly edging away from the water's edge, clutching his shoes protectively to his chest.

Michael's attention was drawn to the water. "What is it?" Michael asked. "I don't get it. Who's Escalonde, and what's with her bath water?"

Merlin paused then whispered, "The Fountain of Youth."

"What?"

"This water is from the Fountain of Youth. That's what's giving her magic its power, its longevity. She really can keep us here for fifteen hundred years."

36

Michael watched as Morgan's magnificent wings carried her toward the east. "Do something!" he yelled.

"I can't," Merlin answered, looking at his watch.

"Yeah, well, I can," said Michael. He looked around and spied a rock; he picked it up and threw it with surprising accuracy at the retreating bird-woman.

The stone clipped Morgan Le Fay's right wing.

She screeched in surprise. The rhythm of her flying was broken; she fell a few metres before regaining control of the massive black wings.

Michael saw the bird-woman wheel and fix her gaze on him. "Oh, oh," he said as he stumbled backwards, away from the diving creature.

Merlin had not seen Michael throw the stone. He was holding his watch and staring at the water. An idea was forming in his mind.

The second hand clicked rhythmically around the dial of his watch. The water swirled rhythmically around the dial of the island. Time was moving. He almost had it — the magical aspect Morgan had missed, the trick that would undo her handiwork. It was right there on the tip of his —

"Aiiieeee!"

The shriek broke Merlin's concentration. He looked up and saw a streak of red and black hurtling toward him.

He threw himself in front of Michael.

Morgan swooped down low over their heads, pulled up sharply, then simply continued on her way, laughing.

Merlin stared. He was amazed at her self-control. Amazed and afraid. Her confidence in her magic was terrifying.

With renewed determination, Merlin turned back to his watch. He closed his eyes and reached his arm out over the edge of the tiny island. With his finger tracing a counter-clockwise circle above the water, he intoned, "Round and round, back and back . . ." He opened an eye and peeked at the water.

Nothing happened.

He tried again, this time lowering his finger enough to almost, but not quite, touch the water, "To undo the spell of Morgan Le Fay, turn the water the other way."

Still, nothing happened.

Merlin dipped the tip of his finger into the water, stirred, and repeated the words.

Michael heard him and came over. "What are you do-ing?"

Merlin frowned at the water, put in his whole hand and tried again.

Again, nothing happened.

He looked up at Michael, "Oh, I'm just trying to change the direction of the Coriolis effect of the Northern Hemisphere — that's all."

"Oh," Michael said and looked at the clockwise-spinning whirlpool. "Didn't you teach us that the Coriolis effect was caused by the rotation of the earth — something we can't change?"

Merlin nodded, called himself an idiot, repeated the words, and stuck his arm in the water up to his elbow.

The water lapped at Merlin's arm; its spray sprinkled his face, his neck, his chest. But the direction of the whirlpool remained unchanged.

"I'll help —" Michael began and reached for the water with his right hand.

"No! Don't touch it!" Merlin yelled.

"Why? You are. Besides, you said it was the Fountain of Youth — that's a good thing."

"Too much of a good thing," Merlin said and waited to see that Michael would obey.

Michael stepped backwards and put his hands in his pockets, "Okay, but if you fall in, I'm gonna grab you — I don't want to stay here for the next fifteen hundred years by myself."

Merlin smiled and turned back to the water. Something was happening. His arm was tingling. He leaned forward and plunged his arm in all the way up to his shoulder. Merlin churned the water with all his might, "I command the Coriolis Force. Time reverse to your natural course."

The waves of the whirlpool crashed into each other with tremendous force as the water tried to change direction. The water broke against the shore of the tiny island, drenching Merlin. Michael jumped back, out of the water's reach.

Merlin pulled his arm out of the water and sat back to watch his handiwork. He and Michael stared as the water of the magical lake started to spin counter-clockwise.

Merlin looked at his wet clothes, felt his wet hair. He watched the waves roll, listened to them rumble; he thought they sounded like doom.

37

Merlin blinked. It was really happening. Not only had the spin of the whirlpool reversed itself, but the water was being sucked down into it. Down and away, back to the earthly paradise, he presumed.

Merlin looked to the sky, half expecting to feel the talons of some horrendous black and red Pterodactyl. But the horizon was clear. Everything was going to be okay. He and Michael watched the water recede. Quickly, at first, then more and more slowly, the unnatural swirl of the whirlpool was winding down, stopping. They looked out over the much smaller, very shallow expanse of gently undulating water.

"Why's it stopping? Why's there still some water?" asked Michael.

Again, Merlin looked up at the sky. Again, he saw nothing. He shrugged, "Maybe the magic's all gone and this is what's left."

"Think we can get across?" asked Michael.

"We have to — before Morgan Le Fay comes back. Her magic's been compromised. She won't be happy."

Michael started for the water. Merlin held him back, "I'll go first."

Merlin stretched his arm out over the water and closed his eyes. He sensed nothing ill, nothing dangerous, nothing that would harm Michael.

The instant that the very tip of Merlin's big toe touched the water, he felt safe. Safe and strong and on the right path. He stepped in with his whole foot then quickly followed suit with his other. He looked down: the water lapped playfully at his ankles. He felt a power, a force — but no threat.

Merlin started to reach a hand back to Michael — he was going to offer to carry him, piggy-back, across the water — when he heard a splash. He turned and saw Michael standing in the water beside him. Words of protection raced to Merlin's lips, but no magic came. The boy was in no danger.

Satisfied that all was well, Merlin started to ford the mini-lake. As he walked, the water rose to his knees, then to his thighs. He looked back and saw Michael, a short distance behind, managing quite well in the calm, hip-high water.

Merlin fixed his mind securely on the shore and pressed on. As he walked, the intoxicating feeling of safety grew stronger, enticing him to slow down, to stop . . .

Merlin shook his head. He tried to clear his mind of the sudden desire to linger. He tried to clear his ears of the unmistakable tone of harp strings. Merlin took a few more steps. The music was irresistible. He couldn't help but turn toward it.

As he turned, he saw that Michael was very far behind — and heading in the wrong direction.

Michael was gliding through the water, listening to the music, moving toward the sound. Ahead of him, something disturbed the water, sending out ripples, like sound waves, on the otherwise serene surface of the little lake.

Merlin reached out a hand in what he hoped would be a signal for Michael to "stop," instead, it seemed more like he was gesturing for Michael to "wait-up".

Merlin watched as the expanding edge of the outermost ripple touched Michael. A thin sliver of light shone from the bubbling centre of the watery disturbance.

Michael stared at the dazzling beam of light as it cut through the water, cut through the air. It seemed to call to him. His feet moved faster toward it in reply.

Merlin couldn't move at all. The water was holding him in calming, soothing waves that whispered repeated assurances that there was no danger. Merlin watched helplessly as Michael moved closer to the bubbles, moved closer to the light, reached out his hand —

The light flared brighter.

Merlin saw the tip of something shiny, something metal, something sharp, rise through the excited bubbles.

Michael and Merlin watched with rapt attention as a gleaming sword pierced the water. The elegant weapon rose to its jewel-studded hilt, revealing a slender feminine hand wrapped surely around its grip.

Clear beneath the surface of the water was the form of a beautiful woman; her golden hair floated easily on the tiny currents of the lake; her emerald and turquoise gown fanned outward. Her eyes were closed. Her expression peaceful. She simply held the sword aloft and waited.

Michael stared, eyes wide, drawn to the sword. He moved through the water easily as if it was helping him, pulling him.

"Wait," Merlin found his voice, but it was an uncertain sound. He felt no danger, and frankly, he wasn't sure if he had the right to interfere.

Michael turned to look at his teacher, "If you can be Merlin, I can be Arthur . . ."

Merlin saw the strength of character in the set of the boy's jaw, the strength of purpose in his calm brown eyes. Merlin said nothing more. Who was he to decide if Michael was ready, if Michael was the one . . .

He watched as his student turned toward his destiny.

Michael took the last step and reached the vision of the lady. In a heartbeat, he reached for the sword. Too late, he saw the gold and silver amulet baring the blood-red stone.

38

Michael knew it was too late to scream. Too late to run. Too late to save himself. He saw the watery vision's eyes open; he saw the golden hair turn black; he saw the tip of the sword aim for his heart. He saw the peaceful visage break into a gruesome smile of satisfaction.

Merlin thought of battle shields, of rubber theater swords, of a scarecrow's stuffing harmlessly spilling out, but nothing happened. Merlin watched in horror as the blade of the great sword thrust up toward the boy's chest.

Merlin tried to move, but the water weighed him down, pulled at his legs, sucked at his feet. He grabbed his legs and tried to force them into action. He heard the scream and froze. The piercing cry echoed off the still water and up into the forest canopy beyond. But the pitch was wrong. Merlin looked up and saw that Michael was not the person screaming.

Michael stood gaping in terrible wonder at the sight before him. A new sword was rising up through Morgan Le Fay's chest. It was Morgan who was screaming.

The sword in Morgan's hand turned to dross as her blood turned the emerald and turquoise dress red.

Michael stepped back. The sword that rose through Morgan's body gleamed with a living light. It sliced the sunlight with a magical precision like perfection, like confidence, like victory.

Morgan's face was dissolving. Her scream waning. Her blood-red form dissipating in crimson ripples. The water ran red for only a moment then changed back to the haunting blue colour of the tiny, unusual lake.

The last thing Michael saw, before the water washed away the memory of her face, was Morgan's expression of utter, incomprehensible, surprise.

Merlin now found himself moving easily through the water to Michael's side.

He stood beside the boy. Together they gazed at a new face. A beautiful, peaceful face beneath the gently caressing currents of the water. The Lady of the Lake continued to hold the new sword aloft — the true sword.

Michael turned to Merlin, "Is it?"

Merlin was enthralled by the Lady's face. Though her eyes remained closed, she seemed to be gazing at him with kindness and deep understanding. In that moment, any doubts that he still might have had, left him. He knew who he was. He knew he was Merlin: always had been — always would be. Merlin whispered, "Yes. I believe it is . . . Excalibur."

"Is it for me?" Michael asked, not taking his eyes off the great sword.

"There's only one way to find out."

Michael paused, "It looks heavy . . ."

"You're strong enough," Merlin said and smiled as his earlier words came back to him, "on the inside — where it counts."

Michael turned away from his teacher toward his future. He looked at Excalibur, bright and full of promise. He reached out to take it.

The Lady of the Lake smiled and raised the sword higher.

Michael's fingers gently closed over the Lady's hand. She released her grasp easily, lightly transferring the great battle sword to the young boy. As the last essence of her magic touch left Excalibur, Michael felt the full weight of the heavy weapon. He stumbled in the water, trying to regain his balance.

Merlin raised a hand to help but stopped himself.
Michael found his footing and hefted the sword, familiarizing himself with its feel. It took two hands, but Excalibur was his.

Merlin smiled. He looked at the Lady of the Lake, she too was smiling in her magical sleep. Slowly, gracefully, she descended beneath the waves, leaving a trail of emerald and turquoise sparkles on the water's pale blue surface.

As Merlin watched, he felt the water grow cold. He looked toward the shore, "Come on, let's get out of this water . . . I'm starting to prune."

Michael smiled and followed his teacher toward dry land. As Michael sloshed through the water, he cradled the sword in his arms like a baby — like a responsibility.

39

On shore, Michael gently laid Excalibur on a bed of dry leaves while Merlin built a fire — the hard way.

Merlin bent protectively over the tiny flame, fanning it, feeding it. He looked up at Michael, apologetically, "There's nothing to eat . . ."

"That's okay, I'm not really hungry."

Merlin nodded, he was tired, exhausted. He rubbed his stomach — an ache had been growing for some time. He looked out over the water; a disturbing thought was forming in his mind.

"What's wrong?" Michael asked.

Merlin looked at the boy. He saw that Michael had taken off his shoes and socks and put them in front of the fire. Merlin shook his head, "Nothing. My stomach's just upset and I'm tired."

Michael nodded. He wasn't tired at all. He was excited — consumed with thoughts of the future, of the sword.

Merlin followed the boy's gaze to Excalibur. The sword was truly magnificent. Merlin looked at Michael and waited. Michael stared at the sword for a long time before he finally spoke, "It's heavy."

"Yes," Merlin responded.

Michael paused again. This time he looked up at his teacher, at his friend, "What am I supposed to do with it?"

"Lead."

"Lead?"

"Wisely," Merlin added.

Michael didn't respond. The enormity of his situation was rising up, threatening to overwhelm him. "What if I can't?"

"You can."

"I'm afraid."

"I know." Merlin started to reach for Michael's shoes, to move them closer to the fire, when he felt a sudden pain in his stomach.

Michael was at his side in an instant, "What is it?"

Merlin patted Michael's shoulder, "Time to sleep."

The boy saw that his teacher was exhausted. Michael looked around — there was little shelter available. He saw Excalibur snuggled in the leaves and quickly went about piling enough leaves together for two more soft, warm beds beneath the stars.

Merlin saw the bed Michael was making for him and smiled gratefully. He wanted nothing more than to lie down and sleep. Merlin took off his watch and looked down at his feet — he couldn't remember what had happened to his shoes.

He looked at his watch and got the distinct feeling that it was battling forward, struggling for every second — as if the drive wheel was trying to turn against the direction of the unwinding spring, as if the spur wheels were trying to reverse their direction, as if the hands were fighting against their inevitable path around the dial — as if the entire mechanism was actually trying to reverse its course.

Merlin looked at the calm water of the little lake and remembered the whirlpool; remembered his countermanding of Morgan's magic; remembered the change in the swirl of the water. Merlin remembered where the water had come from.

He rubbed his stomach. He felt sick, dizzy; he could hardly keep his eyes open. Merlin forced himself to look up at the waking stars. He watched them for a long moment before he spoke, "I won't be here in the morning."

Michael stopped "fluffing" his leafy bed and looked at Merlin, "What?"

"When you wake up, I won't be here."

"Why not?" Michael asked, fear creeping into his voice.

"I think I made a mistake."

Michael stared.

Merlin smiled self-consciously, "When I changed the direction of the whirlpool — when I got wet . . ."

"I'm wet too —"

"Yes," Merlin said, worried, considering, "but you didn't go in until the whirlpool had unwound itself. I think you'll be okay. I mean, I think you'll wake up and it'll be tomorrow."

"And you won't?"

"I think I'll wake up and it'll be yesterday."

Michael's brow furrowed, "That doesn't make any sense."

"I know. But If I'm not here, I don't want you to be afraid."

Michael was afraid now, and his eyes showed it.

"I'll find someone and I'll tell them where you'll be. Just wait here until they come for you. Promise me you won't leave this spot."

Michael paused then gave his promise.

Merlin closed his eyes and sighed with relief. His need for sleep was all-consuming. He wouldn't be able to fight it much longer. Merlin settled heavily onto the bed Michael had made for him. His mind was hazy with sleep, but he couldn't let go — not yet — there was one more thing he wanted to say to Michael. Merlin rolled over and looked at Excalibur. The sword reflected the light of the rising moon.

"Don't get too caught up in your own glory," Merlin whispered.

Michael looked at the portentous sword. He felt like cry-ing. "I need you."

"You'll be fine," Merlin said and knew it was true. He reached out to Michael.

Michael felt the warm hand of a friend on his.

"Remember . . ." Merlin continued, struggling to speak through the billowing cloud of sleep, "remember to light a candle."

"Light a candle? Is that what you do?" Michael asked, trying to keep his teacher awake, hoping to keep his friend with him.

Merlin smiled as the sleep overtook him, "It's what all teachers do . . ."

Dr. Cassandra Westinghouse had just started searching for footprints around John Merlin's abandoned car when a rustling sound told her she wasn't alone. A twig snapped and she spun around.

"Dr. Westinghouse, I presume."

Cassandra stared in surprise. John Merlin was leaning heavily against a young grand fir only a few metres away. She saw that he was deathly pale and clearly in great pain. She also saw that he was alone.

She ran to him.

Merlin let her help him sit down. Cassandra kneeled beside him and checked him over, looking for injuries. Except for his lack of shoes, he seemed to be all in one piece. "Michael?" she asked quickly.

Merlin raised his hand to stop her, "He's okay. Or he will be, day after tomorrow. You must reach him by the day after tomorrow."

She saw that each word was costing him great effort. Merlin gripped his stomach in pain. "I have to get away, far away, as far as possible . . ."

"No, don't run — whatever happened, I'll stand by you," Cassandra said, misunderstanding. "But we have to find Michael now —"

"No!" Merlin rasped and grabbed her arm, hard. "The day after tomorrow — you mustn't find him until the day after tomorrow." Merlin released his grip on her arm and wiped his forehead; the effort was almost too much.

Cassandra looked at him for a long, quiet moment, then asked simply, "Why?"

Merlin shook his head, "You wouldn't believe me."

"Try me," she said, then added as she took his hand in hers, "trust me."

Merlin looked into her eyes. Michael would need her. He nodded, "This is going to sound crazy —" he caught the look in her eyes and almost smiled. "Remember what happened at the Halsey's house?"

"Yes."

"Well, Morgan Le Fay is tracking us, right now — she's going to catch us tomorrow. That's why you can't reach Michael until the day after. If anything happens to change the events, I'm afraid his destiny will be affected . . . my destiny . . ."

"Are you trying to tell me you think you can see the future?"

"No. I'm saying I've already lived it. I went to sleep Sunday night and I woke up today.

"Today's Saturday," said Cassandra.

Merlin nodded, exactly. I'm living backwards. I fell asleep — I had to, I couldn't fight it — and I woke up today, which is yesterday.

"Where's Michael?" she asked.

"He's not affected. He woke up Monday — I hope. You and he should be making your way back by now."

Cassandra let go of Merlin's hand. She wished she had her notebook. "We have to find Michael and then we have to get you to a hospital. We can talk later."

"No, please. Please," Merlin grabbed her hand back, "I don't have much time."

"John, I can see you're in pain. Perhaps there's an internal injury —"

"I'm fine. It's just that I'm too close to myself. Two Merlins can't be in the same place at the same time. Today I'm

155

living backwards — and forwards — at the same time. At least until Sunday night. After Sunday night, I won't be here anymore — I mean I won't be here in your future, but I'll be here in your past, living backwards. Am I making sense?"

The look on Cassandra's face told him he wasn't.

"Please," Merlin begged, "I'm talking to you now — which is happening at the same time as Michael and I are running away from Morgan Le Fay. Please try to understand, to be-lieve me . . ."

Merlin had to stop, to rest, the effort of talking was clearly adding to his pain.

"I believe you," Cassandra whispered. I don't understand, but I believe."

Merlin smiled. "I have to get as far away from myself as I can for the next — the past — thirty years, until — before — I'm born. But I had to see you first: to say good-bye . . . to say thank you . . . and to ask you to watch over Michael."

Cassandra looked at Merlin and nodded. "Where will you go?"

"Europe maybe, or Asia. A teacher can always find work. If not," he gestured at the woods around them, "I can always live off the land for a while."

Cassandra shook her head. It was a lot to accept. But then, so were the events of the fire. "Morgan Le Fay?" she asked.

"Gone, but her magic was terrible — I'm serious, don't find Michael before Monday."

Cassandra paused then agreed to Merlin's terms with a nod of her head.

"Good." Merlin pulled a crumpled piece of paper out of his pocket, "Here, I drew you a map — it's a route that will keep you out of harm's way and still get you there on time."

Merlin watched as Cassandra studied the little map. For the first time he noticed how truly beautiful she was.

"You've been a good friend to me. And a good doctor. I'll miss you."

Cassandra felt a chill as she saw in his eyes that he really was leaving — for good.

"There's just one more thing," Merlin continued, "about Michael . . ."

"Anything."

"Could you keep an eye on him? You know, check on how he's doing, see if he needs any help?" Merlin paused and lowered his voice to a whisper, "We had to walk through water from the Fountain of Youth. I don't know if Michael will be affected, but he's going to need someone to talk to — someone who understands."

Cassandra looked at her long-time patient who had so recently become her friend. "I'll look after Michael."

"Not just office visits," Merlin interrupted, "I mean birthdays and stuff too."

Cassandra smiled at the genuine concern in Merlin's voice. "Yes," she answered simply, "birthdays too — today's mine. I promise I'll remember Michael's."

Merlin smiled broadly. For a moment, his eyes shone, "That's the first personal thing you've ever told me about yourself." He looked around, spied a small, vividly pink flower, its lovely petals growing all in one direction as if blown by the wind. He reached out, picked it, then held it out for Cassandra, "Happy Birthday."

Cassandra stared at the flower. A slow smile spread across her face. She reached out and took the gift. "A shooting star," she whispered, close to tears.

Merlin watched her, curious.

She looked up and smiled self-consciously, "Every year on my birthday," she explained, "for as long as I can remember — I've received a bouquet of shooting stars. No card, no note. Just flowers from a mystery friend. They always made me feel very special." She paused and gently caressed the dramatic petals, "There were times in my life when they were the only things that did."

Merlin smiled, "I'll remember."

41

Michael woke in the morning to find himself on the shore of a small lake, alone. Merlin was gone. Michael turned to where he'd left the sword and had to shield his eyes. Excalibur's polished surface exploded with the morning sunlight. He swallowed. It hadn't been a dream.

A sudden sound startled him. He turned and saw a woman emerge from the nearby cedar grove.

She stopped when she saw him, not at all surprised to find him. "Michael Halsey?"

"Yes."

"My name is —" Cassandra was stopped in mid-sentence by a flare of light. She looked and saw the brilliant gleam of the great sword. She stared and she knew — knew the sword's name, knew the boy's fate. She looked back to Michael.

He shrugged, "The Lady of the Lake gave it to me."

Cassandra took a deep breath. Now she understood why Merlin had been so insistent that she not reach Michael until today. She stared at Michael. Was he ready for this? Was she? Merlin was right, Michael would need someone — someone who knew the truth — someone he could trust.

"I'm Dr. Cassandra Westinghouse," she began again, "I'm a psychiatrist." Michael started to protest but Cassandra raised her hand. "I'm here as a friend. As a favour to a friend. Your science teacher John —"

"It's okay to call him Merlin," Michael interrupted. "It's who he is."

Cassandra nodded, "Merlin asked me to help you —"

"You saw him?" Michael asked eagerly.

"Yes. Saturday —" she stopped and looked deeply into Michael's eyes. "He was with you on Saturday, wasn't he?"

Michael nodded.

Cassandra slowly turned to look at the little pale blue lake. She took a step toward it then stopped herself, "Merlin said something about the Fountain of Youth."

Michael nodded, "It was going backwards when he got wet."

Cassandra turned back to Michael, scrutinizing him closely for any of the symptoms Merlin had presented. The boy seemed neither tired nor in pain. "But not you?" she asked.

"No. I didn't go in until it was standing still."

Cassandra turned back to the water, tempted.

Michael understood the look on her face. "I don't think it works anymore," he said.

Embarrassed, Cassandra turned her back on the tiny silent lake, "Well, let's get started."

"Started?"

"It's a long walk back to my car. Your mom and dad are worried sick about you."

"My mom —"

"Your mom knows the truth, but no one else does." The fleeting image of a boy listening at a motel window crossed Cassandra's mind, but before she could follow the thought, a sunbeam caught the sword's shining blade. She gestured to Excalibur, afraid to say its name out loud, "We can hide it in the trunk, for now."

"Hide it?"

"Unless you're ready to use it."

Michael thought about it. He knew he wasn't ready. But he also knew that the day would come when he was. He slipped off his windbreaker and started to wrap the great battle sword.

Cassandra took off her jacket and offered it to Michael — his coat was too small to cover Excalibur by itself. Michael accepted the jacket and finished wrapping the sword.

With the sleeves securely tied around the blade and the hilt, Michael hefted the heavy weapon onto his shoulder.

Cassandra nodded in the direction from which she had come. Michael turned and started toward the cedars.

Cassandra took a last look at the newly created lake and thought about Michael's future. The journey from boy to man was hard enough — from boy to king would be even harder. But for a boy who had walked through the Fountain of Youth — how long would that journey be? How far would it take him?

Epilogue

Massachusetts, 1928

Merlin the Magician had kept far away from the entire North American continent for the past seventy-five years.

He'd come home to light a candle, and today was the last day. He had started tutoring a boy last spring (or rather, next spring) — it had taken him a while to get the knack of structuring his lessons in reverse order. But today the lessons were finished. He had reached the beginning and there was nothing left for him to do but say good-bye before he returned to Canada.

Looking barely a year older than the day he'd left for Europe, the young teacher stood outside the large door of the impressive home for the final time. He knocked and the door opened. A servant showed him into the study and asked him to wait — treating him like a stranger.

Merlin looked around the familiar room, at the furniture, at the books, at the photographs. He paused at one picture in particular — the smiling face of the boy he'd been tutoring — the boy he'd come to care so much about — the boy who was about to meet him for the first time. The boy who reminded him so much of another boy: a boy named Michael who hadn't even been born yet.

Merlin closed his eyes and sighed. Living backwards was very hard. He had no way of knowing what had happened to Michael in the future; yet he knew exactly what would happen to the boy he was about to "meet" today. Behind him, the door to the study opened. Merlin turned to see the boy, "Jack," standing beside his father. Merlin smiled sadly and said, "Hello," knowing it was good-bye.

The older man came forward to shake Merlin's hand and said, "Hello, I'm Joseph Kennedy." He reached back to rest his arm lightly on the boy's shoulder, "This is my son, John — John Fitzgerald Kennedy."

Appendix

The Legend: Once upon a time, there was a boy named Arthur who was raised by a wise old wizard named Merlin. The land in which they lived was under attack from invaders on all sides. With a little magical help from Merlin, Arthur demonstrated his right to lead his people by pulling a sword out of a stone. This sword proclaimed Arthur's right to rule, but it was a different sword — an enchanted sword named Excalibur, given to him by The Lady of the Lake — which gave him his power in battle.

With Excalibur in his hand, and Merlin at his side, Arthur defeated the invaders and reigned over an idyllic time of peace. During this time, his brave knights used their strength to protect the weak, to ensure justice for all, and to pursue noble quests. Arthur fell in love with and married Guenevere while Merlin became enchanted by a sly new pupil, Morgan Le Fay. But after two long decades of peace, this magical kingdom called Camelot began to crumble.

It was under attack from the outside by invaders and from the inside by betrayal and deceit.

In one final, glorious battle, all was lost. Arthur was killed, Excalibur thrown back into the lake, and Merlin trapped for eternity beneath the earth by Morgan Le Fay.

Lost but not forgotten, Arthur's world of enlightened peace, nobility of purpose, honour and justice, shines across the centuries . . . as does the promise that one day, when he's needed most, Arthur will return.

The History: When the invading Romans finally abandoned their occupation of Britain in A.D.410, they left behind a population of Romanized Christian Celts who called themselves Britons. Soon after the Romans left, the Picts and the Scots began attacking the Britons. They were joined by Germanic groups called Angles and Saxons. These invaders pushed the Celtic Britons into the far west part of Briton. But there was one young British general who stood firm against the invading armies. His name was Ambrosius Aurelianus. Some sources believe his nickname was Artos, meaning "the bear", and that he was probably about fifteen years old.

After three years of fighting, he finally defeated the Saxons at the battle of Mount Badon and successfully held them at bay for twenty years while the lands under his protection prospered. This heroic young warrior became the basis for the legend of King Arthur and his Knights of the Round Table.

It is also believed that Arthur had a trusted advisor named Merlin who also served as his bard and historian.

Throughout Medieval times, Arthurian Tales were very popular and became embellished with magic and romance. Today, many people still enjoy reading stories about King Arthur and Merlin.

(Note: see bibliography for sources
and further reading.)

Bibliography

Andronik, Catherine. *Quest for a King — Searching for the Real King Arthur.* New York: Antheneum, 1989.

Ardley, Neil. *The Science Book of Gravity.* Toronto: Doubleday, 1992.

Ardley, Neil. *The Science Book of Light.* San Diego: Harcourt Brace Jovanovich, 1991.

Bains, Rae. *Simple Machines.* New Jersey: Troll Associates, 1985.

Barber, Richard. *The Arthurian Legends.* New York: Barnes & Noble, 1993.

Berger, Melvin. *Switch On, Switch Off.* New York: Harper & Row, 1989.

Blackwood, Alan. *Musical Instruments.* England: Wayland, 1987.

Brandt, Keith. *Electricity.* New Jersey: Troll Associates, 1985.

Royston, Angela. *Machines in Action* — Pulleys and Gears. Chicago: Heinemann Library, 2001.

Dambrosio, Monica and Roberto Barbieri. *The Early Middle Ages.* Milwaukee: Raintree Pub., 1990.

Catherall, Ed. *Exploring Sound.* England: Hove, Wayland, 1989.

Catherall, Ed. *Exploring Electricity.* Hove, England: Wayland, 1989.

Challoner, Jack. *Hands-On Science.* New York: Kingfisher, 2001.

Coghlan, Ronan. *The Illustrated Encyclopaedia of Arthurian Legends.* New York: Barnes & Noble, 1993.

Cole, Joanna. *The Magic School Bus — Inside the Human Body.* New York: Scholastic, 1989.

Cole, Joanna. *A Frog's Body.* New York: William Morrow and Company, 1980.

Fichter, George S. *The Animal Kingdom.* New York: Golden Press, 1968.

Grant, Neil. *The Medieval Word.* New York: Oxford University Press, 2001.

Hart, Avery and Paul Mantell. *Kids Make Music.* Charlotte: Williamson Publishing, 1993.

Kerrod, Robin. *Earth and Moon.* North Mankato: Smart Apple Media, 2000.

Knapp, B.J. *Science in our World: Waves and Vibrations.* Toronto: Grolier, 1993.

Lauw, Darlene and Lim Cheng Puay. *Science Alive — Electricity.* St. Catharines: Crabtree Publishing, 2002.

Parker, Steve. *Step into Science: Light.* London: Granada, 1985.

Ravielli, Anthony. *The World is Round.* New York: The Viking Press, 1963.

Rice, Chris and Melanie Rice. *How Children Lived.* Mississauga: Fenn Publishing Company Ltd., 1995.

Riordan, James. *King Arthur.* New York: Oxford University Press, 1998.

www.ingramcontent.com/pod-product-compliance
Lightning Source LLC
Chambersburg PA
CBHW030257130626
46549CB00002B/569